Theme and Variations

by Robert M. Ellis

ISBN 978-1-4476-8074-1

Other books by Robert M. Ellis

Philosophy
A Theory of Moral Objectivity
The Trouble with Buddhism
A New Buddhist Ethics
Truth on the Edge

Poetry
Truth on the Edge

For details of these books see http://www.lulu.com/spotlight/robertupeksa and also the author's website http://www.moralobjectivity.net

Theme and Variations - Contents

Note

This book aims to represent the spirit of a number of different thinkers through the ages, and to set each of them a similar test. However, in doing so it has taken considerable liberties with them as historical figures. The book should be taken as a work of fiction rather than history or biography.

Theme: The Buddha

As soon as Kisa woke up she realised something was wrong.

She turned over automatically in the straw to find Siddhattha and give him her breast. In the half-light she groped for her baby, but found a bundle that was heavy and inert. Her heart suddenly pounding, she gently shook him: there was no response. His face was still and set. His flesh was cold and rigid.

Kisa sprang up with a cry, clutching her baby to her. Surely he just needed some milk, or a cuddle? He would come round. Not her first-born! Not the fine, healthy baby that all her neighbours had admired!

Her husband stirred, then went back to sleep. But her mother-in-law, across the room, sat up at her cry.

"Kisa, what is it?"

"It's Siddhattha! He's cold. He won't move!"

Her mother-in-law came up to her and felt the child.

"I'm sorry, Kisa. He's dead." In the dim morning light Kisa could just see her eyes, which were full of compassion. "Sometimes the gods take them and we don't know why. It happened to me. Three of my babies died before Vasettha was born."

Kisa looked at the earthen floor.

“You will have more,” her mother-in-law went on.

In a few moments a succession of ideas passed through Kisa’s mind: her joy at the birth of a healthy boy, after her painful labour, only a few weeks before; her belief that he would grow into a fine man; intense mortification at the joy that had been suddenly denied here; then, finally, guilt. It must be a punishment for something she had done wrong. But what?

“It’s a mistake!” Kisa cried abruptly, “He can’t be dead. I don’t deserve this!”

With that she tore out of the house and down the street, still clutching her dead baby. She didn’t know where she was going, only that she had to get away and find someone to fix this mistake. She cried out and muttered to herself as she ran.

“Kisa! Why are you making so much noise?”

A familiar harsh voice had hailed her from a rooftop. She turned in confusion. It was Dona, the corpulent Brahmin who employed her to clean his house. He sat on his roof-top every morning to recite prayers to the rising sun.

“It’s my baby,” she managed to say, “My mother-in-law says he is dead.”

She looked up towards the Brahmin for a moment, but did not meet his eyes. She recalled how Dona had unsuccessfully tried to seduce her about a year ago, though he had resentfully left her alone after she became pregnant.

“Ha! All you deserve, girl, for neglecting your duty! It is your own karma!”

She could not defy him, but nor could she accept his judgement. She fled further down the street and squatted beneath the banyan tree by the well, moaning softly to herself. She became wrapped up in her own self-pitying world for a while, abstracted from all contact with others. Some women of a different caste, who were drawing water from the well, ignored her.

Finally there came a touch at her elbow. It was Rupa, her closest friend since childhood. She seemed to have heard the news. “I’m sorry,” She said.

Suddenly the torment from which Kisa had fled re-awakened in her. “He’s not dead!” she cried, “I don’t deserve this! I’m not guilty!”

“Perhaps it is a sin from a past life, not from this one,” Rupa gently suggested.

“No, no, I have done no sin.” Here she thought again about the sin she had avoided with Dona. “I will find a real holy man who knows this, that I have done no sin. He will understand, then he can make Siddhattha all right again!" She was suddenly resolved, her heart beating fast again.

"But he's dead.... " began Rupa, then realised that her friend was in no state to accept this. Then an idea occurred to her. "I do know a holy man...."

"Who? Where?" demanded Kisa eagerly.

"He came to the mango grove yesterday, a very famous holy man. They call him Buddha, and they say he can read people's minds and do great miracles. But the Brahmins hate him. Dona will forbid you to see him."

"In the mango grove?" The hairs prickled on the back of Kisa's neck.

"Yes."

Kisa immediately ran off, still with the bundle in her arms, straight for the mango grove outside the town. Rupa called after her, warning her of her parents' and employer's disapproval, but soon saw it was no use, and went back to her work.

When Kisa arrived at the mango grove, the Buddha and his followers had just risen from their morning meditation, and were about to go into the town on their alms-round. One of the followers intercepted her as she entered the grove.

“Please could I see Buddha?” she begged, “It’s important.”

“Not now,” said the follower, “The Master is about to begin his alms-round. Come back this afternoon.”

But the Buddha was already coming towards them, and Kisa ran away from the follower and up to him, falling on her knees before him.

“Please,” she said, “My name is Kisa, and they say my baby has died, but it’s all a mistake. I’ve done nothing wrong! Please can you bring my baby back to life?”

She was shaking, too nervous to observe the Buddha’s serene, compassionate expression, or the animation of his disciples, who were gathering around them. Bring her baby back to life? The Master did not do cheap tricks like that. This woman ought to know better than to ask him for such a thing.

The Buddha pondered for a few moments, then at length he said, “I teach the way to end all suffering.”

Kisa’s spirits rose. Did that mean he could end hers?

“But there is only one way I can suggest to end your anguish.”

He paused. Surely that meant he could bring her baby back to life!

“Fetch me a grain of mustard seed. Just one single grain will do. But it must come from a house where no-one has ever died.”

She immediately leapt up. “Yes sir, I’ll do that. It won’t take long. I’ll be back very soon, sir.”

Mad with anxiety, she thought that the Buddha would soon depart on his alms-round, and she must get the mustard-seed straight away before then.

She ran to the nearest house, close to the mango grove. She did not know the people there, but surely they could not refuse her simple request?

A woman opened the door.

“Please – I know this is strange – but could I have a grain of mustard seed? The Buddha’s about to go on his alms-round and he needs it for my baby.”

The woman looked extremely puzzled, and did not move.

“Oh, and there mustn’t have been anybody died in the house. The mustard seed must come from a house where nobody has died.”

The woman smiled mirthlessly, “Then I’m sorry, I can’t help you there. My father died in this house only a few months ago.”

Before she reached the next house, Kisa had begun to realise that the requirement of someone not having died in the house was likely to be important. This time she began with, "Please could you tell me whether anyone has died in this house?"

"Yes, miss, my granddaughter died here only last year."

"The gods took my mother from here five years ago."

"My uncle died here only last week. You must know him, he sold vegetables in the town. Have you not heard?"

"Died? People die all the time. Why do you ask?"

After twenty houses, Kisa was once again distraught. How could she get back to the Buddha in time now? She went back to the well and sat down again beneath the banyan tree. She looked again at the frozen face of her child. People died all the time. And he was dead.

The words of the Buddha came back to her: "There is only one way I can suggest to end your anguish," he had said. She suddenly realised that he hadn't actually promised to bring her child back to life. Of course, if she had thought about it she would probably have realised that lots of people die, but she had been too upset to think. She began to realise, though, that Siddhattha was one of the people who had to die. Maybe she didn't deserve it, but the fact was that he was dead. As acceptance gradually filled her she slowly began to weep tears of relief.

After a while she got up and went back home. The little body was cremated by the river bank that very afternoon, with Dona officiating.

That evening, as the sun was sinking, she returned to the mango grove to see the Buddha again. She found him deep in discussion with his disciples, but they broke off as she approached. She bowed respectfully before the Buddha, with a heavy heart but composed mind.

"I did not find the mustard seed, sir, for I believe there is not one house in the whole town where no-one has died. I believe you sent me on that errand so I should learn that I'm not the only one. Am I right?"

"You are right, my daughter. It is good that you have understood this."

"I have another question, sir."

"Please ask it."

"You said that you teach the way to end suffering. Please teach me what that way is. How is it possible to end suffering?"

"I cannot take away old age, sickness, withering and death, but I can help you overcome the anguish these things bring with them. The first step in that way you have already gone, which is to recognise that suffering exists."

“Did I deserve it? Is it a punishment?”

“Maybe, maybe not. That is not important. But once you have accepted that suffering exists, you can begin the Path which ends anguish. The Path is a long and difficult Path, but if you become my disciple, I will teach you more of this Path.

The Greeks

Variation 1: Plato

Scene: A dinner-party in ancient Athens. On the table are chicken-bones, bread-crusts, grape-stalks etc. A servant is pouring wine from an earthenware bottle into the cups of the guests. Socrates, a booming bearded philosopher, is talking merrily with the host, a man called Glaucon. Another servant comes in hurriedly and speaks to Glaucon

Glaucon	It seems that there is a young woman at the door wishing to speak to you, Socrates.
Socrates	To me? Well, let her in then.
Glaucon	But we can't let a woman into a dinner party!
Socrates	And why can't we let a woman into a dinner party?
Glaucon	Because...she'd spoil the conversation with her triviality and chatter, and distract the young men who should have their hearts set on higher things.

Socrates — My dear Glaucon, do you really think it's likely that a woman has come to interrupt a dinner party for that kind of purpose? Would she really appear at this time of night just to make trivial conversation and distract the young men from your beauty? Isn't it likely that she'd have a more important purpose?

Glaucon — I didn't say anything about *my* beauty. Oh, all right, I suppose it must be something serious. But why didn't she send her husband? *(to the servant)* Bring her in, then.

Servant — Are you sure, sir?

Glaucon — Yes.

After a pause, Kisa appears at the door, holding a dead baby in her arms.

Glaucon — Oh good heavens, the servant didn't say you were bringing.... (*stiffly*) Can I help you, madam?

Kisa — I want to speak to Socrates.

Glaucon — He is here, but could I ask why you have to bring in that...that *body.* After all, this is not a funeral, you know, just an ordinary dinner party.

Kisa	He's my son.
Glaucon	He may be your son, but that doesn't mean you have to bring him in here, surely?
Kisa	THIS IS MY SON, AND THE GODS HAVE TAKEN HIM UNJUSTLY FROM ME!
	Everyone stops talking and turns to look at Kisa, stunned.
Kisa	Now where is Socrates?
Socrates	I am Socrates.
Kisa	Sir, they tell me that you are the wisest man in Athens.
Socrates	(*bowing*) They flatter me. If I am wise it is only because I know the extent of my own ignorance.
Kisa	However it is that you are wise, you must be able to give me an answer to this question. They say that the gods are just, yet they have taken away my child from me, who is only a few weeks old and has done nothing wrong. They say that the gods are just, but they have broken my heart, when I have done

nothing wrong. I have always obeyed the laws, obeyed my father and my husband, looked after my family and done my duty without complaint. And yet they punish me thus! Please Socrates, if you are wise, can you tell me how the gods can allow this?

Socrates (*after a pause*) Well, first you must know that my wisdom, such as it is, only allows me to ask questions, not to answer them. I am not wise enough to find the answers all by myself, when there are others who know the answers so much better than I. So first I must ask *you* a few questions.

Kisa If you wish.

Socrates Well, first you tell me that the gods do nothing unjustly. Is that right?

Kisa That is what I have been taught, and what I believe.

Socrates Very well. And then you also tell me that your child is dead. Well, that is very clear. We can see that he is dead. But then you also link these things together, and tell me that the gods are unjust in taking away your child. Is that correct?

Kisa	Yes, that is correct.
Socrates	It is this that we should examine, I think. And you say that the gods are unjust because neither you nor your baby have done anything to deserve punishment?
Kisa	That is right.
Socrates	So would you say that the gods have punished you and your baby by bringing about his death?
Kisa	Yes.
Socrates	So death is a kind of punishment?
Kisa	That is right.
Socrates	Then let us look at what death is. When we die, our soul is separated from our body, is that right?
Kisa	So I have always been taught. I have no reason to doubt it.
Socrates	And which gives us more suffering: the soul, which has no pain, or the body, which is subject to pain?
Kisa	The body.

Socrates So separating the soul from the body releases us from pain?

Kisa Yes.

Socrates But a punishment, I would have thought, involves the infliction of pain, is that right?

Kisa Yes.

Socrates But in this case we have agreed that death, which is separating the soul from the body, gives no pain, and in fact releases us from pain. So death cannot possibly be a punishment. Am I right?

Kisa I suppose so.

Socrates And if death cannot be a punishment, the gods cannot possibly have given it to your son unjustly. Is this not true?

Kisa I suppose it must be.

Glaucon This is all very well, Socrates, but you have bewildered the poor woman by only talking about how death can be a punishment *for the baby*. Perhaps it is just a release for the poor little chap, who never did anything wrong: unless it can be wrong to suck your mother's milk and cry when you are hungry, in which case we are all wrong-doers. But what about for the woman herself? *She's* still alive, and suffering the torments of the body. Surely her son's death is a pain for her, and an unjust punishment from the gods?

Socrates — I was just coming to that, Glaucon, but you have forestalled me. Very well, let us examine whether the baby's death is really a punishment for the mother. We have agreed already that a punishment must involve pain, yes?

Kisa — Yes.

Socrates — So what is the pain involved in the death of your son?

Kisa — How can you ask? Isn't it obvious? The grief of losing a baby I love, the loss of him growing up, him not becoming a man, my husband not having an heir, a feeling that I have not done my duty as a woman: all of these things.

Socrates — Very well, but you also know that your son's soul is separated from his body, and that he is freed from pain. Is that not right?

Kisa	Yes.
Socrates	And if you love your son and he is freed from pain, should that not be a source of happiness for you?
Kisa	Yes, I suppose so.
Socrates	If he is freed from pain, is this not of greater importance than these drawbacks to you, especially given that you can have another child to give your husband an heir and so on?
Kisa	Yes, I suppose so.
Socrates	So, in giving you greater happiness, how can the gods have punished you? Rather you should feel that they have given you a blessing. Far from wanting your son back, you should be glad that the gods have taken him!
Kisa	(*sighs*) It is hard, but I suppose you are right.
Glaucon	Good, I'm glad that has been satisfactorily resolved. Now perhaps you can go and bury that, er, *body* in the proper fashion, and we can get on with the dinner party, as it is proper for gentlemen to do.

Variation 2: Pyrrho

My brother-in-law Pyrrho and I had always got on very well, before he joined Alexander's army and went to India. He was away a good many years, and most of the family had begun to think he was dead, when he finally returned. After the immediate relief of welcoming him back it quickly became apparent that he was very much changed, and full of strange ideas. He'd been a bit of a philosopher before he left, but then it had only been a sort of hobby. When he was in India, though, it seemed he's been in contact with the gymnosophists, those Indian philosophers who combine thinking with strange exercises, can make themselves dead for three days then come back alive (by all accounts), and constantly debate whether to believe in one thing or many things or none at all.

But Pyrrho came back with the belief in nothing at all, or so he said. He said it was healthy to doubt and that we'd achieve peace of mind by giving up our beliefs. So he wouldn't agree with what anyone believed at all. He'd say that there was no proof either way, whatever anybody claimed, and any proof they offered was never good enough. If you believed in anything at all then he'd say it was "dogmatism".

What's more this wasn't just a passing phase. It's true that some young men get like that for a while, just to show they're independent of their fathers and teachers, but after they've made their point they generally go back to believing what most sensible people believe. But Pyrrho was a man of mature years, who took his scepticism very seriously. He gathered disciples who used to meet at his house, he wrote books, and he debated with other philosophical types in the agora.

I'm a sensible and tolerant man, as I'm sure my neighbours will agree, but it's now that Pyrrho began to irritate me. It was harmful to a family's reputation when a man went off the rails like that. Rather than disown him, I used to try to catch him out. When he was eating his dinner I asked him if he believed whether his dinner existed, and if he didn't why he was eating it. He said he had no reason either to believe or to disbelieve in his dinner, but given that there was no proof either way, it was better to "acquiesce in appearances".

I was in this phase of trying to catch him out, when suddenly our son died. He was only a few weeks old. Many families lose several babies and don't worry too much about it, but this one was special because of the circumstances. My wife, Kisa, had seemed to be barren most of her life, and although we'd wanted children, she'd never managed to have any, however much we implored the gods for a child and made the right sacrifices. We'd completely given up hope when at last the gods responded. She was nearly forty by the time she finally found herself pregnant. So the child was our first-born and probably only son, for we didn't believe Kisa would ever manage to get pregnant again. We called the child Alexander, after the old emperor (which Pyrrho, the child's uncle, seemed to like), and cherished him more than any other child. But then, one morning, we woke up and found, inexplicably, a little cold corpse where there had been a healthy baby the night before. Kisa, as you'd imagine, was mad with grief, weeping and wailing.

At this point, when we were both lost in grief, who should drop by but Pyrrho, wanting to borrow some money (he didn't believe in money, but it seemed he still wanted to borrow the appearance of it). When he heard the news he was upset too, of course. He had no children of his own, for he wasn't even married, but he obviously looked forward to the role of a fond uncle. To do him credit, he did say a few kind words when he heard the bad news. But some perverse whim seized me at that moment, perhaps due to the distortions of my grief. I decided to seize the occasion to try to show him how ludicrous his scepticism was, once and for all, and how it was really an insult to take it seriously and get it mixed up with real life, when real life involved suffering like this.

"What do you make of this, huh, with your clever scepticism? There's your sister beside herself in her room because she's lost the only child she'll ever have, the one hope our hearts were set on, and all you can do is not believe in things! This is real life, Pyrrho, where people suffer, not your useless philosophical discussions!" All my grief came out as a rage against Pyrrho and his scepticism. I think I went on like this for some time, as far as I remember, but Pyrrho just sat there, calmly, listening. He never got upset about anything, and this is one of the things that was so irritating about him.

When I had finally completed my tirade, Pyrrho got up and asked if he could see Kisa. "I don't see why she should want to see you, you good-for-nothing disgrace to the family! How are you going to help her at a time like this!" I grumbled, but I went to fetch her nevertheless. Kisa was obviously still very upset.

We sat down in silence with a cup of wine, but then Pyrrho began his response. "Look, Kisa, I'm very sorry for you both at a time like this. My sympathies go out to you, and I feel very sad myself. But your husband seems to think that scepticism makes it worse, whereas I think that it's at times like this that it's most helpful. I wanted you to be here to hear my explanation."

We nodded mutely and let him go on. I had blown out all the energy I had at that moment and suddenly felt empty, with no more resistance in me.

"Can't you see that the reason we get upset at times like this is because of our fixed views about things? We believe that there's justice in the world, and that death should only come at the right time. But doesn't this prove that these are deluded beliefs? For all those who say there's justice in the world because they worked hard and were rewarded, there are others who are punished for no reason, as you are. For all those who die at a ripe old age, convinced that the gods are on their side, there are others, like my nephew, who die at the time that seems least just, before they have even had chance to do good deeds or ill in this life. So why should we believe that the world is just? Just let go of that idea and you have no need to be upset, for no injustice has been done. The gods can hardly have cheated you, for they may not even exist!"

"May not even exist!" cried Kisa. She seemed to have suddenly woken up from a reverie, and could hardly have been following what her brother was saying, until then suddenly she reacted to the last sentence with rage. "You're not going to say that my little baby's soul may not even exist either!"

"Exactly," went on Pyrrho, "We don't know whether there is a soul that goes on without a body, or just a body, so that's it when you die. We just don't know. So what's the point of hanging onto these things? Just relax."

"Relax?" echoed Kisa in distant disbelief.

"Yes, relax: just chill! I mean, I know you're all upset, and so am I, but when you start to really reflect on it there's nothing really to be upset *about*."

"How dare you!" cried Kisa, suddenly getting up with animation, "How dare you add such insult to our grief at a time like this! Nothing to get upset about, indeed! Call yourself a brother? Get out of the house this minute! I never want to see you or your scepticism again!" She picked up a broom and started to jab it towards her brother, as though to weep him out of the house.

Meanwhile I sat there astounded. It was me who had been angry at first, but then gained some control over myself. But I had never seen Kisa quite as angry as this.

"But Kisa, I'm only trying to help. I'm your brother..."

"Get *out*!"

Pyrrho was forced to retreat and leave the scene of his ill-judged philosophising. He tried to come back and make peace later that day, but Kisa, true to her word, would not let him into the house and wouldn't speak to him again. She has completely refused to do so ever since.

I, for my part, have not held quite such a strong grudge against him. He didn't choose the best day to try to turn us into sceptics, but he meant well, and he is my brother-in-law. Sometimes we acquiesce in the appearance of a cup of wine together down at the tavern. And I sometimes think that just relaxing might not be such a bad idea, given all the trouble this philosophy business causes.

Variation 3: Aristotle

Gentlemen, let us continue our examination of the virtuous life from where we left off last week. As you will recall, we have been examining the different types and categories of virtue which together help us to become ideal characters, and work towards the goal of *eudaimonia*, the ideal life or moral perfection of a human being. We have been looking at intellectual virtues, which aid us in our judgement and have been acquired through study, and at practical virtues, which are a matter of training and habit.

This week I want to look at a very special and important virtue which helps to bridge the gap between these intellectual and practical virtues. It is a practical virtue which we develop through good habits and training from childhood, just as in the case of the other practical virtues like courage and patience, but it is also vital to stop our intellectual judgements from being warped. I am speaking, of course, of *temperance*, the ability to make clear judgements unclouded by pleasure or pain.

Gentlemen, it is impossible to over-state the importance of this virtue for society, for the state, for philosophy both physical and metaphysical: in fact for the whole of human life! If there is a corrupt politician who puts the interests of his family before those of his country, it is due to lack of temperance. If there is a compulsive gambler who ruins his whole family with his obsession, it is due to lack of temperance. If there is a soldier who, captured by the enemy, reveals important information under torture because of his fear of pain, to the ruin of his comrades and his country, it is due to lack of temperance. If, on the other hand, there is a virtuous citizen, universally admired and just to all, one of the strongest characteristics of such a man is that he will not be swayed from his path by a greedy desire for pleasure, nor by a corrupting and cowardly fear of pain.

Perhaps we all know at least some examples of those whose judgement has been corrupted by pleasure or by the desire for pleasure: the gluttonous old man, who, having abandoned the higher pursuits he had in his youth, thinks only of the pleasures of the table, and cannot judge when to stop eating, however bad it may be for his health; or perhaps the adulterer who ruins his family life and his reputation through his failure to control his sexual behaviour. The corruptions of pleasure are easy to imagine and to report.

But what of the corruptions of pain? Some have argued that, far from corrupting the judgement, the fear of pain may sharpen or clarify it, as in the case of the schoolboy afraid of his master's punishment. But the schoolboy is still in the process of early training. Those who are immature, or criminal, or slaves, may well need their judgement shaped in the right way by judicious punishment. But a citizen of ripe years should be able to judge in a balanced way for himself; and for him, the fear of pain removes the independence of the judgement which he himself should make, casting him down to grosser levels of thinking when he is capable of higher and subtler ones. Only the virtue of temperance offers any protection against this.

So a virtuous man should be able to remain unswayed by the prospect of pain. He will still remain honest, for example, even under pressure of blackmail. Even in a more extreme case, that of present pain, his judgement should remain unclouded, as in my earlier example of a soldier under torture. That example reveals the relationship between temperance and courage, for we also require courage to maintain faith in our own judgement when subjected to pain.

What of a virtuous woman? As I have stated before, women are less rational creatures than men. In some ways, then, they are in the same category as the immature or as slaves, in needing direction rather than developing an autonomous characteristic of temperance. We may be justified in punishing a wayward wife who fails to control herself. On the other hand, I am inclined to think that some women show signs of developing temperance, so we should encourage them in this. Where such matters are doubtful, we should rely on our observations of the capacities of individual women.

In this connection, I would like to mention a remarkable case that I came across a few years ago, of a woman who developed a remarkable degree of temperance through her response to suffering. Her name was Kisa, and her mother was a Spartan: which perhaps explains the pains which her mother took in bringing her up after the manner of the Spartans, educating her almost as much as a boy. She was a spirited girl, and married an officer in the army, who was killed in the wars soon after, leaving her pregnant. At this point her husband's family, who had always been suspicious of her because of her Spartan ancestry, disowned her, inventing a story that she had dishonoured the family by being unfaithful in her husband's absence. Her father had died in the same campaign as her husband, fighting alongside his son-in-law, and her mother had returned to Sparta, leaving her alone in the world with a small child. Many suggested that she, too, go to Sparta, following her mother, but she rejected this suggestion as she identified too much with the city of her Athenian husband and father.

As if this were not misfortune enough, more suffering was in store for her. Quite soon after the birth of her baby, the child suddenly died. The young woman was mad with grief, not knowing what to do with herself. As I had known her father slightly, and as she thought that a philosopher might be able to give her some good advice in her plight, she came to me, still clutching the body of her dead baby which she would not let go of. I listened first of all while she railed against the gods and her misfortune.

With most other women I would have told her to obey her husband or her father, but she had none. I realised that, being responsible for herself as a man is, in this case she would have to develop some of a man's virtues.

"Listen!" I said, "You have the training from childhood to overcome these griefs, so all you need to do is calm your mind, apply your wisdom and your good sense. Do not try to escape from your despair like a coward, nor give yourself up to it, but face it with courage. Above all, do not let this pain cloud your judgement. Reflect that many other women have lost their children in infancy. You have a good and steadfast character, and you do not need to yield to this calumny from your parents-in-law, nor to the madness of this grief that is afflicting you. You do not need to blame the gods for your misfortunes, for your life is your own. Set aside your griefs, and find yourself a new husband, or an occupation such as virtuous widows use to support themselves. You may still develop a good character, have moderate means, and live a full life."

She seemed to be calmed by this advice, and, whether it be due to my advice or to her mother's upbringing, she soon forgot her grief and settled down. She took up a humble enough occupation, spinning and weaving, but she seems to be happy enough to this day. She seems to me to give remarkable proof that temperance is possible, even for a creature as irrational as a woman. But the role of the right upbringing and education in all this, in training her in the right habits to cope with the greatest of afflictions, must not be underestimated.

Hmm. I have dwelt on this one example more than is my custom in these lectures. But perhaps it has been necessary, to illustrate the importance of temperance to everyone in daily life. I was going to go on to discuss justice, but perhaps we will leave that until next week.

Variation 4: Zeno

Scene: Zeus's court on Mount Olympus. Zeus is sitting on his throne, with Hera next to him. Hermes is in attendance nearby, as are various other gods, goddesses and demi-gods.

Zeus — Hermes?

Hermes — Yes, my Lord.

Zeus — It's a long time since you gave me an update on intellectual affairs down there, as opposed to politics and wars and such like: and you know how I like a good argument. What are the philosophers up to, eh?

Hermes — Well, you've heard about Aristotle, haven't you, sir? I told you about him the other day.

Zeus — Oh, *him*! Boring old sod, just gives lectures all the time. He hasn't got into any interesting arguments, has he?

Hermes — Only with Zeno.

Zeus — Zeno? Who's he?

Hermes — He's started a new group called the Stoics, because they meet in the Stoa for their discussions, my Lord.

Zeus So what's he arguing with Aristotle about?

Hermes About whether an arrow can ever reach its target, my Lord.

Zeus Eh? But of course an arrow can reach its target, provided it's been shot right. What are they on about?

Hermes Well, Zeno says that if you only used reason to tell you whether an arrow would reach its target, you would conclude that it never would. We would think that an arrow would first travel halfway to its target, then half the remaining distance, then half of the remaining distance, and so on to infinity. This is just a way of saying that space and time are infinitely divisible, so no motion at all can ever be completed in space or time.

Zeus (*unusually thoughtful)* So, let's think. If I chop you in half, then in half again, and again and again and so on to infinity, I'll never get to the end of it.

Hermes May I remind you that I am a god, my Lord. You cannot chop gods in half. Still, if you did that to a mortal, it would certainly be true in theory, yes. In practice, though, you'd get to a point where you couldn't see the pieces, and your blade would be too big to cut them.

The senses will tell you a different story from reason alone.

Zeus So that's why an arrow will reach its target, too. You can see it does!

Hermes Zeno argues that you have to rely on the senses, because reason leads you into contradictions like these. The senses tell you that the universe is one and cannot be divided up in this way, because everything works together as a seamless whole.

Zeus And so it does, thanks to us gods, of course! Seems to be a clever chap, this Zeno. But I'll bet that boring old fool Aristotle has some objection. What is it, then?

Hermes He thinks that reason and the senses must work together. He *doesn't* think that space and time are actually infinitely divisible, only potentially so, so the arrow *can* reach its target according to both reason and the senses. Instead the world is made in such a way that we can sense it *and* reason about it. What reason tells us will be in harmony with what the senses tell us. He says that Zeno has just been reasoning wrongly.

Zeus Ha! If you ask me, it's Aristotle who's been reasoning wrongly. How does *he* know that reason and the senses will always give the same result? Has he reasoned all the things that are to be reasoned? How does he know that some funny piece of geometry won't come up with a result that doesn't fit what we see? I've a good mind to make one: that'll flummox him! Anyway, that's enough of Aristotle. Tell me more about this Zeno guy. What else does he believe?

Hermes — That Nature guides us as to what is good. Because we must use the world of the senses as our guide, this is the way we come to know what's good.

Zeus — Ah! But what about evil? How does he explain it when even I, the Lord of the universe, kill my father and go about ravishing mortal maidens?

Hermes — That when we are evil we haven't understood what is truly natural, but rather followed our false desires, and used false reason to justify them.

Zeus — Does he think that *I* don't know what's truly natural? I rule over it all, by Zeus!

Hermes — I think he would say that your actions reveal that you do not, my Lord.

Zeus	Ha! And how will he like it when I throw a thunderbolt at him for his impertinence?
Hermes	He will bear it calmly, I'm sure, my Lord. He won't let pain or fear disturb him, but will carry on unperturbed. He would even meet death with dignity, and end his own life when the occasion demands it.
Zeus	A remarkable mortal! But I wonder if he's really as strong as you say. Could he really explain away all the misfortunes which we, the gods, throw at mortals? Won't he start thinking of things as good or bad according to his desire instead of ours, as all the other mortals tend to do? Won't he just blame us?
Hermes	I'm sure he will not, sir.
Zeus	Let us put him to the test, then! Let's see.... Let's send him some really difficult piece of human suffering which is full of pain but completely natural; let's send him a woman whose baby has died, suddenly, for no reason. It's her first and only child, and she's mad with grief and curses the gods.
Hermes	I could take on that appearance, sir. This sounds fun!
Hera	No! I hear this plot! If you really must go baiting this philosopher, then at least send a

being who really knows what it is like to suffer in that way. No male could ever really know what it's like to lose a child. Let me go! I will take on the appearance of this woman: let's call her Kisa. I will really feel her anguish, so there's no way that philosopher will be able to explain it away. Otherwise Hermes will just be unconvincing and let him get away with it. But I'll be really frantic! More grief-stricken than the most tragic playwright could depict!

Hermes But I want to watch the fun!

Hera You can come too. Take on the appearance of the dead child and I will carry you.

Zeus (*laughing*) A stiff test indeed! I doubt if any philosopher will be able to calm a goddess's grief.

Exeunt Hera and Hermes

****

Some time later they reappear. Hera looks disappointed and Hermes victorious.

Zeus Well? Did the philosopher pass the test?

Hermes Yes, with flying colours.

Hera Not for lack of effort on my part.

Hermes Indeed, she was more of a tigress than a woman: a mad, frantic tigress attacking the injustice of the gods with tooth and claw. She wanted her dead cub brought back to life.

Zeus But Zeno managed to calm her?

Hermes He was impregnable. However much the storm raged, he never lost his temper, and never lost an inch of his faith in a just world. In the end, he just wore her down with calm and reasoned argument.

Zeus So – she gave in?!! (*looking in amazement at Hera*)

Hera Defeated by a mortal! I am sick! *(she exits)*.

Hermes How could she not? Is it not clear as the starry sky? Can it not be read in the flight of birds and the swaying of trees in the wind? How could the reign of the gods be anything other than just? All it takes is for a mortal to see this clearly and he cannot be faulted. For things to be otherwise would be against Nature.

Zeus Of course! (*laughing*) It would also be against Nature for the female to defeat the male, would it not? The senses tell us that, too, no matter what warped reasons or the desires of women may make of it! I wish good luck to this philosopher. Long may his doctrines rule!

Hermes — *(cautiously)* But, er...do you not know how long they will rule anyway, sir?

Zeus — Oh, yes, of course! A good long time. But of course it will some day be the will of the gods for a less sensible doctrine to prevail: just to make things more interesting.

Variation 5: Epicurus

16th Thargelion

Today we had a new visitor in the Garden. Her name is Kisa. She arrived in quite a distraught state, poor woman, clutching her dead baby. It seems that she had some strange idea that the Master could bring it back to life, and she hadn't really accepted that it was fully dead. It took some time to calm her down enough to explain that the baby is only made of atoms, and once it's died it's died, there's no way to bring it back again. I'm not sure she really understood, because she kept going on about its soul even when we assured her that there are no souls. Still, at least she allowed us to take the baby away to be buried after a while.

The Master said that she should stay here a while at least, while she gets over the shock of her misfortune. She will need a great deal of patience and care, poor woman. The Master asked me to keep a special eye on her, and she's staying in the guest room which is next to mine.

17th Thargelion

Kisa was making quite a disturbance last night, weeping and wailing. I went into her room to try to soothe her. She went on and on about her poor dead baby, and how he must still be alive somewhere and would come back to her. She'll never get over her grief so long as she keeps hanging onto these ideas, I'm sure. But there was no possibility of persuading her that night, she was too far gone in her distress. Eventually she just fell asleep from sheer exhaustion and I tiptoed out of the room.

She went on sleeping for much of the following day, but woke up in time for dinner. Then she still seemed a bit dazed, but started to tell us a bit about her life. She comes from Crete, it seems, and has had many hardships; cruel parents, and a husband who left her. The death of her baby seems to have been the final straw which led her to some sort of breakdown. Still, at least she turned up here, and we're able to help her.

18th Thargelion

Today I was able to have a more detailed discussion with Kisa, with her in a calmer state of mind. She seems exceedingly grateful to have been taken in by the community like this, but I explained that kindness, hospitality, and relieving distress, are part of our practice here. This led to her asking more about the Master's teaching. I skirted around the issue of her baby not having a soul for now until I could be surer that she was ready, but I explained how we give priority to pleasure.

She seemed surprised, like many people, to learn that the Master teaches that greater pleasure is gained through virtue than through debauchery. But she seemed impressed. It was a new discovery for her that pleasure could be a good thing rather than a source of temptation to be rejected. If only more of the world was ready even to make this simple discovery!

But I could see she was still feeling too much anguish to go on with this conversation for too long, so I bid her good night, with a final assurance that it was all right for her to recognise her pain, for that was the only way to overcome it and feel pleasure again. I felt some satisfaction that we are making progress with Kisa. Perhaps she will even become a new sister given time.

19th Thargelion

I was busy in the bakery all day today, and didn't have much time to speak with Kisa. Still, she seems to be settling down. I even saw her smile once.

20th Thargelion

Now that Kisa is looking so much more relaxed, I felt I really should speak to her about the Master's teachings on atoms and the material body. I managed to have a chat with her in the courtyard after dinner. At first she was confused and suspicious. She couldn't understand how we could value friendship and hospitality and other kinds of higher pleasure, and yet not believe in souls. It also still upset her to think of her baby just being a material thing and not having a soul.

But after a while she began to come round, and said she'd think about it all. She said she was happy to value virtuous pleasure, but didn't see why believing in atoms and not the soul was so important. I tried to explain, but perhaps I got a bit impatient after a while, and didn't make a very good job of it. I suggested that she ask to see the Master himself. He's very busy with his books, of course, but still happy to see people from time to time. She said she'd think about that too.

21st Thargelion

Today I felt the time was ripe to ask Kisa if she wanted to stay on in the community. I said that she was welcome to stay on and become a sister, and I was sure this would help her get over her grief and find a new life. I told her about how fulfilling I find it living here, living in harmony with others and following the Master's teaching, and how much I'd enjoy having her here. We'd have to find her some regular work of course, but she could start that gradually as she was recovering. I could do with some more help in the bakery.

She said she wasn't quite sure, and needed some more time to think about it. But I have high hopes.

22nd Thargelion

This was a disappointing day for me. Just when Kisa seemed to be settling in so well, and I was sure she was going to stay, she suddenly decided to leave. What's more, after all the care and effort I've taken with her, she didn't even stop to thank me or say goodbye!

The Master came to find me in the bakery to explain that she had come to see him, to tell him that she was sorry, but she didn't believe her baby was only atoms, but that he had a soul, and he was calling to her and would come back to her. The Master tried to argue with her, and explain why believing in the soul only led to pain, but she was stubborn. Apparently she said that she was very grateful to me for my friendship, but that she felt she had to leave now, and couldn't face saying goodbye to me.

People can be very strange sometimes. They're outwardly relaxed and seem to be taking pleasure in things, but within they are still deeply confused and act in irrational ways. I would be inclined to be angry about Kisa's behaviour, but the Master reminded me that anger leads only to pain and we must keep calm at all times.

The Christians

Variation 6: Jesus

As Jesus passed through Capernaum, a crowd of people gathered who had heard of his signs and wonders. Amongst them was a woman called Kisa, who was bearing in her arms her dead child, only a few weeks old. She fell at Jesus' feet, saying "My Lord, I beg you, bring this child back to life!"

Moved by her faith, Jesus helped her back to her feet. "Woman," he said, "Give the child to me." She handed the child to him, and he bent low over it and gently said "Awake!". The child then stirred and looked up at Jesus and laughed. "Take him back and care for him," said Jesus to the astonished woman, "For he was only asleep. We will all wake thus on the Day of Judgement." The woman departed with her child, filled with happiness and giving thanks to God. Soon news of this wonder spread through the whole district.

Later the disciples questioned Jesus and asked him, "If it is God's will that some live and others die, why do you bring the dead back to life, as you did with Kisa's child?" Jesus answered, "It was his mother's faith that brought the child back to life. It is God's will that those who have faith will live and those who do not will die. The resurrection of Kisa's child today was only a foretaste of the greater resurrection of the dead on the Day of Judgement that is coming."

Variation 7: St. Paul

To my brothers and sisters in Christ in the Church of the Polygonians, Paul sends his greetings.

I am sending this letter by the hand of a good woman whom I entrust to your care. Her name is Kisa, a woman of noble birth and upbringing but many misfortunes. When she came to see me first, in the city of Athens, she carried the body of her child, whose life the Lord had taken away. She was full of awe and sought my advice.

She was gladdened when I told her that the child was with God, and would rise again in his spiritual body at the time of the second coming of the Lord, to be judged with the living and the dead. She was also gladdened when I told her that all could be saved who had faith in the Lord Jesus Christ, both men and women, and that she could join in his ministry in preparation for the Kingdom.

She questioned me further by asking why God sends such misfortunes as the death of her child on those who have not sinned. I told her that all have sinned since the sin of our first parents, so that none of us are free from sin. God in his mercy has sent the Lord Jesus Christ to save us from the fruits of our sins, but not because we are without sin. Under the law we are guilty, but faith and love will set us free. The proper wages for sin is death, unless we accept Christ's salvation.

At these words, she was struck as though with a blow, and she fell to her knees, possessed by the Holy Spirit. She told me later that she had heard the voice of the Lord at that moment, telling her to repent of her sins and accept Christ. Then she swooned, but when she awakened declared that she wished to accept the Lord Jesus Christ as her saviour, and asked for baptism. I rejoiced with her at the happiness that the Lord had brought out of her misfortunes.

We then prayed together over the body of her dead child, and gave it the right burial. After this she wanted to stay with me, but I explained to her that God had given me the great work of being an Apostle of the Lord Jesus Christ, and I needed to follow his bidding, to travel to new cities and new countries and spread his word there. She fell to her knees and said she would follow me to the ends of the earth, and be my wife, if I wished it, or otherwise my servant.

I was moved by her faith, but knew that her sudden devotion to me was not just heavenly, but earthly, and was born from her distress. I explained to her that whilst those whose flesh is weak are married, to save them from sin, it is better for those who are able to devote themselves wholly to God and be wedded only to the Holy Spirit. I thought it best not to stay with her too long after this, lest this hopeless earthly love grow stronger yet.

This is why I must ask your aid, my friends, knowing you to be a faithful and hospitable church holding fast to

Christ. I thought it best to send her to you, for I know that you will care for her as a sister while she recovers from her distress and learns the Christian life. I advise you to teach her carefully before you baptise her, for at present she has more inspiration than understanding, and sometimes her ideas are confused. I know you will make her welcome in Polygonia, and find her some suitable occupation to earn her livelihood.

Please give my greetings to my great friends Titus and Demetrius, and especially to that faithful couple, Aramis and Chloe, who were so hospitable to me during my stay in Polygonia.

Variation 8: St. Augustine

When little Marius died I fell into a rage. Why I was suddenly so enraged that time I'm not sure, for I had lost children before. Perhaps it was because there had been so many: Fabricius, Johannus, Tertius and even little Calpurnia had all been taken away so young. Then even Stephanus, who had survived to the age of ten, was a sickly lad, and no-one really knew whether he would reach manhood. Then there had been the pain and torment of my mother during her last illness, and the behaviour of my good-for-nothing husband. It seemed that everything in my life was suffering, pain, and drudgery, and when I got a little joy, like Marius, who was such a lovely baby, then even that would be taken away from me. Sometimes I would wake up in the morning with a bruise on my face from one of *his* drunken outbursts the night before, still feeling exhausted and with my heart sinking at the prospect of another day, but I would look down at Marius as the sun shone in through the window, and he would look at me with a smile of such sweetness and innocence that life would suddenly seem bearable, even happy, for a few moments. Then one day all that was suddenly taken away from me again. I woke up and looked down, and his little body was cold and lifeless.

Something snapped in me that morning. All the neighbours, and my father, and my husband, and the priest, all told me that it was the will of God, and that I should accept it, for we deserve no better in our sinfulness. Suddenly a defiant spirit rose up in me:

perhaps it was from Satan, I do not know. This death could not be the will of God, not if God is loving as they had told me. I was seized with rage, and picked up Marius's stiff little body, carrying it with me. I went straight to the priest's house and got him out of bed. I showed him Marius's body.

"What sort of just and loving God is this?" I shouted at him, "Is he only just and loving to men, that he makes women suffer so much? How can he take away this boy, the sweetest-natured child I ever knew, and the fifth of my children to die?"

"I'm sorry for you, my daughter," said the priest, "But at least the child was baptised. He will go to heaven, do not doubt it. But do not harbour sinful thoughts against God. God is loving and merciful and wise. We do not know why he has taken away your child, but have faith in Christ and you will be saved."

"He cannot be loving and merciful," I cried, "not taking away this many children! Or perhaps he is, but he does not really rule the earth. Perhaps there is also an evil God, as the Manichees say."

"Hush, my child! Do not utter such blasphemies! The Manichees will go to Hell for their false beliefs, cursed by God! He is the only ruler of heaven and earth, believe me. Satan works his mischief, but only by God's leave!"

"Why does God give him leave, when he could stop this mischief! He cannot be a loving God!"

"I do not know the answer to such questions, child."

"Then who does?"

"Only perhaps the great and the learned, such as the bishop. Our bishop is a holy and learned man, who was once a Manichee himself, until he was converted by the great bishop Ambrose of Milan. Only he, perhaps, of holy Christians I have met in this land, could give any answer to such questions."

"How can I see the bishop, then?" I demanded, not really expecting an answer.

The priest sighed. "You, a peasant woman, go to see the bishop? Well, it is true that he will speak even to the most humble, I am told, when they ask about the faith. I advise you just to put aside these sinful thoughts, which are beyond your station, to bury the child and go back to your daily business. But if you must see the bishop, you must go to the city of Hippo, find the bishop's house, and ask for an audience."

I set off at once, for the rage still possessed me. I persuaded the neighbour's son, a young lad of fifteen, to take me to the city in his donkey-cart, for it was twenty miles to Hippo. I think he was awe-struck by my going around in a rage carrying a dead baby, for I wouldn't let go of the little corpse. It was almost a talisman. If I could look at his little frozen face, the fires of anger would not go away, whereas I knew that once I let go and let them bury him, everything would go back to how it usually was, and my husband would probably beat me up then if I tried to go to Hippo.

It was night-fall by the time we got to the city and found the bishop's house. The servant at the door said that the bishop wouldn't give an audience so late, for he would be at his studies and his prayers, but he would see me in the morning if I came back. We had no money for an inn, so we slept in the cart in the square, with me still hugging the corpse as though it was still alive, and the lad muttering in his sleep. I was hardly able to sleep at all myself, I was in such a state of agitation.

I was almost afraid that my anger would have left me by the morning, but I had only to look at Marius's little body for it all to come surging back. This time, when I enquired, the bishop would see me. I left the lad behind to look after the donkey, and was led by the servant into a large hall. At the end of it was a throne on which the bishop sat.

I wasn't sure what to do. Should I bow as though he was a king? But to my surprise he got up from his throne as soon as he saw me, and immediately came up to me and shook my hand. He saw the dead baby and immediately looked in my face with sympathy and concern.

I was astonished by this approach, for I had expected someone a bit like the priest only even more pompous. I don't think I'd ever met anyone who showed love so much. It shone through in everything he did.

“Welcome, my daughter.” he said, “Have you come to see me about this poor child, whom I see the Lord has taken away from us?”

I almost gave up at that point. Perhaps there could be a loving God, if he had appointed such a loving man. But then I recalled my anger and stuck fast to my purpose.

“My Lord,” I began, “I came to ask you about.... The priest said that you would talk to people about matters of faith, however humble.... I wanted to ask about whether there could be a God of love who does such things as take my baby away from me like this. He is the fifth of my children to die, sir, the fifth. And he was the sweetest of them all, and gave me such joy in life, just for a few moments sometimes, sir. And now he’s been suddenly taken away. I don’t think I can believe that there’s a God who rules all the world who does this, sir. There must be an evil god who’s just as powerful, at least, sir.”

“Hm.” From being radiant and welcoming the bishop now became thoughtful. He moved away from me and started pacing up and down. “What you are asking me is a very important and very difficult question, my daughter. It lies at the heart of Christian faith. So no, I do not blame you for asking it, nor do I think it a sin to ask it. It is a matter which many learned fathers of the Church have given much thought to, and indeed something I have given much thought to myself. I wonder how I can best explain it to you.”

He paused, and I stood there astonished. Nobody had ever taken my awkward questions so seriously before.

“There is one Father of the Church,” he said, “Called Irenaeus, who thought about it in this way. He said that sin and evil is all for our good in the end, and even Adam’s sin was a good sin in the end, a happy sin. For it is only by sin and by evil that we come to know good. So if he were to meet you with your dead child, my daughter, he would probably say that God allows such suffering so that, by contrast, you can recognise good.”

He looked at me enquiringly, as though he wasn’t sure whether I would understand, but I answered him immediately: “What good does this help me recognise?” I cried, brandishing little Marius’s corpse, “I cannot see any good that I come to know by this!”

“Perhaps, when you go home, you will come to appreciate the life of others more, because the child is dead?” he enquired, “Perhaps you will appreciate the life of your other children?”

“All dead,” I replied, “Apart from one, who is sickly and likely to die before he becomes a man.”

“Or your husband?”

I grimaced, “A good-for-nothing scoundrel and drunkard! I wish *he* had died instead of the child. Then I could marry again and choose a better man. *Then* there might be a loving and just God!”

"Come, come," said the bishop mildly, "I'm sure he must have some good qualities too, or you would never have married him in the first place. Still, I'm not sure that I'm convinced myself by Irenaeus's way of seeing it. It seems to me that he's in danger of saying sin is good, which can never be right, or it would not be sin."

"So what do *you* believe, sir?"

"I believe that our sufferings are due to the sin of Adam and Eve. For it was then that paradise was broken, that evil began. As human beings, together, we brought suffering upon ourselves. Man was cursed with drudgery and toil, and woman with pain in childbirth, as it says in the scriptures. But along with that there have come other sufferings, too: wars, famines and pestilence. Why, your sufferings, my daughter, though great, are not nearly so great as some have had to bear. You may have lost your children, but you still have enough to eat, you have health, you have liberty. All these sufferings; famine, disease, enslavement, brigands, barbarian invasions, all are the common lot of mankind. God appoints these sufferings justly, not because of our particular wickedness, but because of the sinfulness we are born with, the original sin, which was given to us by our first ancestor."

"But I was not born sinful!" I cried, "I have done nothing wrong! Instead I have borne many injuries. I obeyed my father when I was a girl, and obey my husband now, however good-for-nothing he is, but he still beats me for it. I go to church and try to say my prayers, however much I doubt. I do not deserve this punishment from God."

"No, no, I am not saying it is your individual sin, my daughter – though I'm sure you are not faultless, whatever you say – no, it is the *original* sin that every human being has inherited that is the cause. It is the sin of Adam and Eve that brings this suffering upon us, spoiling our originally perfect nature and marring God's perfect creation."

"But why should I be punished for another's sin! Surely that cannot be just?"

"Think of it as like a debt left behind by your grandfather. Supposing your grandfather died owing money to a neighbour. Would it not then be just for you to pay the bond in his place?

I thought for a moment, "Only if I could do so without starving my own children, " I replied, "He might have got it by gambling or anything. I'd pay his debts within reason, because I'm his descendent, but not if I had to suffer too much for it. That wouldn't be just."

The bishop sighed. "You have a very sharp mind, for a peasant woman, and you are stubborn. I can see that I'm not going to convince you. But in the end, after all the arguments, we simply have to have faith. We do not know the mind of God or his great design. What seems to us to be evil may well be good in the greater scheme of things."

I looked at him squarely. I don't know how I had the courage, looking back at it, to say what I said next, but it was as though I was possessed, that day, holding that little corpse in my hand. "No, sir, I'm not convinced. And I don't have faith any more, if I ever had it. I don't think I deserve to be punished for what Eve did such a long time ago, at least not this much!" I looked at Marius again and it renewed my nerve. "And I don't think good will come of it either, not from this much grief. Maybe a little bit, but not this much."

"So are you telling me you don't believe in God?"

There was a silence, a deadly hush, as the bishop and his servants all waited for my answer.

"No. At least not in a God who does this to me. He can't rule all the world and love everyone too."

There was an outraged gasp from the servants, but the bishop remained calm. "So are you going to leave the Church?"

"Yes, sir. I think I'll become a manichee or a pagan. I think that might suit me better."

"Then I'm afraid you will go to Hell. I'm sorry to hear of your apostasy. But you are free to sin in this way if you wish: God made us all free."

I left the hall somehow prouder, on the crest of a wave. I looked in Marius's eyes for the last time, and knew that everything had changed. I could never go back to my old life if I gave up being a Christian. I passed the body of Marius to the astonished lad in the donkey-cart.

"Please take him home and have him buried. Give the body to the priest and he'll arrange it."

"Are you not coming back, miss?"

"No, I must learn to live some other way. Tell my husband that I am not coming back, and that he deserves this for all his ill-treatment."

"But where are you going, miss?

"I do not know. Leave me."

The boy looked at me with utter incomprehension, then slung the body of the baby into his cart, took the reins of his donkey and drove off.

Variation 9: St Theresa

Last night I had a dream sent by God. It was a vision of Christ.

First he showed me the wounds in his hands and feet and side so that I could know him for sure. “I am the Son of Man, the one who suffers,” he said.

Then he beckoned me, and I followed him. He led me into a wonderful garden. It was surrounded by box-hedges, and the warm air was full of the scent of herbs and the sound of bees. The sun was shining, and the paths were bordered with roses.

Christ led me along a path, beckoning. After a while we came to a young woman sitting on a bench ahead. She was dressed well, had sleek long black hair, and would normally be said to be beautiful, but her face was contorted with grief. She was holding something in a bundle and looking at it, which seemed to arouse her grief, but at first I could not see what it was.

Christ beckoned me around behind the bench to look over her shoulder. She seemed not to be aware of our presence. Over her shoulder I could see what the bundle was: a baby, but it was dead. Now I understood her grief completely. It seemed all the more poignant because she was not some care-worn matron, but a beauty whom one might normally see delighting some fine young man's heart. She seemed only just old enough to be a mother, and I somehow knew at once that this had been her first child. I also knew that unlike most women, she had too little strength and too much sensitivity to go on having children after this first loss.

Then Christ appeared on the other side of the bench, in front of her. Still she did not seem to see him, absorbed in her grief. He held out his hand, and from the wound on his hand a single drop of blood oozed out. The drop of blood fell onto the head of the baby, then suddenly the baby vanished. The woman started, and suddenly she saw Christ before her. She was afraid, but Christ said to her, “Bring your suffering to me, for I suffer with you. Bring your suffering to me and I will give eternal life.”

He beckoned the woman and she got up and started to follow him, and I followed too, observing, or so it seemed. We went out of the garden between the hedges, and then seemed to be in a graveyard. But in this graveyard the graves all seemed to be made of glass, like windows. Beneath the glass we could see skeletons, all writhing around as though in torment as they lay in their coffins. Some of them still had flesh on them which was rotting. “Do not be afraid!” said Christ, for the woman was terrified. Strangely enough, though, I did not fear any fear myself because of Christ’s presence, and was filled with compassion for the woman.

We came to a place where the woman’s baby was buried, and it seemed as though time was speeded up, for we saw the flesh rotting quickly and the bones appearing beneath. The woman was even more terrified, but Christ turned to me. “Console her” he said.

I knew exactly what to do, for Christ taught me without speaking any words. I embraced her and held her close against me, so I could feel the beating of her heart. Gradually the wild beating slowed down, and it seemed that as it did so, so did my own heart, for our hearts beat as one. The baby had become a skeleton in the grave, and it seemed we could now look at it with acceptance.

As soon as we reached this state of acceptance, embraced in divine love, all the skeletons around us ceased to writhe and lay still. Then all the lids of the graves opened, the skeletons gradually gained flesh and clothes again, and began to climb out. Suddenly I felt intense happiness and love, for all the dead were living again in Christ.

Then Christ appeared in the sky in glory, surrounded by dazzling light, and with him were God the Father in his majesty, and Mary the Mother of God, and choirs of angels surrounding them singing the praises of God.

Then all the dead who had risen from the grave began to ascend towards God, and with them were I and the woman. We were all filled with divine ecstasy, and giving thanks to God for our eternal life now given.

I woke up in that state of ecstasy, feeling at one with Christ, who is my husband, and the suffering woman, who is like my daughter. As I go about my business during the day, I have only to think of them, and their faces come before me vividly, and I am filled with happiness, so vivid was that dream. I give thanks to God that I am gifted with such visions, for they come to me through his grace alone, and not through any merit of mine.

Variation 10: Kierkegaard

Dear Miss Kisa,

Many thanks for your letter, which I found most moving. I am touched that you should want to write to me to ask for advice in your sad situation, and fully understand why you have been dissatisfied with the answers you have been given by your local clergy and by the established Church. However, in many ways I fear that I am not the best person to advise you, given the nature of your situation and of your feelings, for I am a lifelong bachelor, and know little of the feelings of women or of children. As you may know, I was once engaged to a young woman called Miss Olsen, but felt obliged to break off this engagement when I realised that I was not at all suited to married life. Nevertheless, I sympathise with your situation as much as I am capable within my narrow bachelor's heart, and will do my best to advise you as I may.

First, you are right, of course, not to be satisfied with the old theological answers. The kind of suffering that you have encountered cannot, and should not, be glibly explained away either by appealing to a necessary contrast with the good (in the manner of Irenaeus) or to the sin of Adam (in the manner of Augustine). Your suffering in particular cannot be rationalised in this sort of way, for it is not due to any kind of human sin, nor does it seem that it will necessarily help you to appreciate the good things in your life. Also, neither of these lines of argument is adequate to explain the sheer amount of suffering that someone in your position has been through. A woman's instincts are specifically made more tender and open to the babe she nurses, it seems, by a perverse God who wishes her to suffer all the more when the baby dies: some justice, indeed! You do not need this death to love and cherish the baby in the first place, for nature led you to do so, and if the death was punishment for some sin, whether yours or another's, it would be far in excess of what is required for the purpose. A God like this would seem to be like one of those vicious sea-captains one hears about, whose absolute power over their crews goes to their heads, and they go about ordering hugely disproportionate punishments, such as keel-hauling a man for climbing the rigging too slowly!

So, no, one cannot rationalise this suffering and make it part of a theological system, for belief in God is not rational. But, to answer the other part of your letter, where you express the intense conflict you feel between a desire to believe in God and the sense of his injustice, I do not believe that this is a reason for not believing in God at all. It may be a reason for giving up your belief in this old, rationalising God, the God like a cruel sea-captain. The belief in such a God is far better left behind anyway. Rather, one should have quite different motives for believing in God. Instead of having *reasons* for doing so, it should be a leap of faith.

I cannot give you any *reasons* for taking a leap of faith to try to persuade you to it, nor should I try to persuade you in any other way. But perhaps your suffering, and your desire to believe in God and to love God may be the very things that lead you into that leap. One is led into a leap of faith by desperation, by the feeling that there is no ground to stand on anywhere else, for one is sinking into a quagmire. But although one may be desperate and driven by suffering, one must make that leap with a full sense of responsibility. One must *choose* God, or what one believes in is not really God at all.

In one of my books, Fear and Trembling, you may have read about the choice made by Abraham. This seems a very important example to me, and very relevant to your experience. You must know the passage in Genesis at least: God commands Abraham to sacrifice his son, and Abraham is so full of faith that he is willing to do it. Finally, just as he is about to raise his knife, an angel commends his faith and bids him stay his hand, providing an animal to sacrifice instead. Now, the example of Abraham is stronger than yours, because he does not just have to accept the death of his child apparently at the hands of God, as you must, but even do the deed himself. So the leap of faith God is demanding of you is of the same sort, just slightly less extreme, but in both cases something that you love very dearly is staked for God. You have to *choose* to love God more than that thing you love so dearly, that dearly beloved child. If you do this, I am convinced, you will find that the God you love as much as this is indeed a God worth loving.

You may ask how you know that it is really God himself who calls you to that re-ordering of priorities. The answer is simply that you do not *know*. You have to choose to believe. We have already chosen to believe in other things at earlier stages of our lives, though we may not have admitted that any choice was involved. We chose to believe in the rules our parents set us, or in the morals of our society. We have never had any final proof that these were right either, but we chose to believe them because they helped us make sense of our lives. To choose to believe in the real God, rather than God the despotic sea-captain, is the final and the highest choice that we can make.

I do not know if you are ready to make that choice, so I cannot advise you to do it. If you are not ready, you will not be making a leap of faith to the real God but to something else, some rationalisation of the human mind. But perhaps your sufferings and your doubts have purified you, so you have gone beyond what the earlier, more child-like stages of religion can give you, and are ready to take that final step.

If you are ready to take that step, you must be ready (and I fear this may shock you) to plunge the knife in, as Abraham was ready: to decide that your faith in God is more important than your attachment to the baby. Yes, it is almost like hardening your heart to murder, for you have to move beyond all your attachment to ethics and to the world being "just" by human standards. To make sense of the world in a truly religious way you have to be ready, at least in your heart (not literally, of course) to do violence to the morality that people hold dear.

Have I shocked you sufficiently? No, I imagine that you have probably gone beyond being shocked after the experiences of grief that you describe. My experiences have been very different, of course, but I too had to feel that God had deserted me in order to fetch him back. We must travel through the valley of the shadow of death in some way before we reach true faith.

I hope that his advice, for all its limitations, is of some use. I imagine that it will either be a lot of use or (more likely) none at all. Most of all, though, remember that the choice must be yours alone. Do not rely on me, or your family, or the Church, or anyone else, to make it for you.

Yours sincerely,
Søren Kierkegård

The Enlightenment

Variation 11: Descartes

Scene: Night-time in Descartes' room in his country house. Descartes is alone and paces up and down, soliloquising. The room is lit only by a candle. A noise of wind and rain outside.

Descartes — So, I am beginning to see it at last! There must be a reason why the world is proven to exist. For I know that *I* exist as I think these thoughts now, without the slightest doubt, even if this room is a dream. But if I by necessity must exist, all that I think clearly and distinctly, using my reason, must exist too, as certainly as I do.

(Descartes pauses, stroking his beard, then resumes his pacing.)

And in amongst those things I must know with certainty using reason alone, must be the existence of God. For God is by definition perfect, and he cannot be perfect if he does not exist! A being that did not exist would be less than perfect. Besides, where could my idea of God, this perfect being, come from, other than from a perfect being! Yes, God must exist. What's more, I need neither Church nor scripture to tell me so. The Perfect Being exists by reason alone.

(*Pauses again, then resumes)*

So, if the Perfect Being exists, it must also be in his perfection to be good, for how could he be perfect and not good? But if he is not good, then he does not deceive me, and, having power over the world, would not let me be deceived – at least, not completely. Maybe there could be the odd mistake here and there, but he wouldn't let me live in a complete dream-world. So, this room must be real! The world must exist! I have it!

(A knock at the door)

Go away, I'm thinking!

(Another knock)

Look, you can't just disturb a famous philosopher like this. I'm having important thoughts! I've just worked out a theory which is going to show that science is true, and change the whole way of thinking in the Western world! Go **away**!

(A servant's head pokes round the door. Her expression indicates that she doesn't take her master's protestations very seriously.)

Servant — I'm awfully sorry to disturb you, sir, but it's an important matter.

Descartes — What could be more important than proving that the world exists?

Servant — But you can do your philosophy any time, sir, and a young woman's arrived at the door, sir. She says she must see you, sir.

Descartes — See me! At this time of night, when I'm thinking! Out of the question!

Servant — She's in an awful state, sir. She's soaking wet from riding out in the rain, and ever so angry and upset, and...and she's carrying a dead baby, sir.

Descartes — A dead baby? What the devil is going on? Did she give her name?

Servant — Kisa, sir. An odd name, but that's what she said.

Descartes — Kisa...? Kisa.... *(Pauses, then remembers)*. Very well, you'll have to let her in.

(Servant exits, and shortly afterwards Kisa enters, carrying her dead baby)

Descartes — Kisa! What do you mean by coming here like this? I thought I asked you to stay in the town and never to disturb me here! Have I not given you enough money to meet your needs?

Kisa — Money! Will money pay for this? *(points at baby)* Will money bring your dead son back to life?

Descartes — Have you come here just to tell me that the baby is dead? Well, I am sorry to see it, but it is not very surprising. Babies do die, often, you know. You could have sent word from the town by our usual method. You did not have to come here to tell me this and disturb me. I am engaged in important thinking.

Kisa — *(outraged)* Important thinking! So is the death of your son not important to you?

Descartes — If he had been older, yes, even though he is illegitimate. But he had not yet reached the age of thought. He did not yet know that he existed. So, his death can be the cause of a little regret, perhaps, like the death of a dog or a horse, but no great funeral orations. I do not think it is a just cause for great displays of grief, no.

Kisa Great displays of grief! Well, I think *I* have cause for great displays of grief, even if *you* think your son is worth no more than a dog or a horse! Not only do you seduce me and get me pregnant dishonourably, promising to marry me then changing your mind; not only do you try to hush the whole matter up by paying me off and keeping me in secret at a distance; not only do you not care for me at all, despite the love I once gave you, but only your cursed philosophy.... I could bear all that, perhaps, and I have been bearing all that, whilst I had my child, my beloved Jean, so much sweeter than his father. At least I could love him and forget my woes, but now – now he is dead. I have no more reason to live.

Descartes Well, look, I am sorry. You know I cannot marry you, for I am married to philosophy and to science. I have explained all this. I think I have done my best, for I am an honourable man, whatever you may say. We will bury the baby, and then you can do whatever you wish. You can continue to have whatever money you need.

Kisa — I have told you, I do not need money! I need my baby back!

Descartes — He is gone, Kisa. You must accept it, for it is God's will.

Kisa — God's will! I thought you didn't believe in God! How can you go about putting reason first before the Church, and then claim it is God's will that the child is dead?

Descartes — Ah, but now I do not need to just *believe* in God, for I *know* God is there. I have only just understood it. That is why I did not wish to be disturbed, Kisa, for I have just realised how to prove the existence of God and the world through reason alone.

Kisa — *(mocking)* So now that you have reasoned your way to God, despite a total lack of faith, you can tell me what his will is! Anyone would think you were God yourself!

Descartes — I am not God himself, but I do know for a certainty, through reason alone, that he is all-powerful and that he is good. For he is by definition a perfect being, and a perfect being must exist by definition, or he would not be perfect. He must also be perfectly powerful and perfectly good, and all that passes in this world must be good. He could never possibly deceive me about this, for then he would be less than perfect. It would be like a triangle with only two sides, it could not be conceived of! So I know that the death of this child is in accordance with God's will, and that it is ultimately good, as clearly and distinctly as I know that two plus two equals four.

Kisa — But only your overgrown, bloated reason tells you this. For those of us who still have humanity, who see with our eyes and feel with our hearts, the death of this child is terrible.

Descartes — You should not depend on your eyes, much less on your heart! Women are too soon moved to depend on mere senses and emotions. These things we perceive and feel, they are constantly coming and going, full of tricks and illusions. Things are often other than what they seem, and the feelings we have about them vanish like the morning mist!

Kisa — I cannot be deceived about what I feel. Do I not know that I feel it?

Descartes — Yes, you do. But you do not know that what you are feeling corresponds to any truth. Using reason, however, you find out what is true: eternally, absolutely, incontestably true!

Kisa — I do not believe in your eternal truths. Once it was eternally true that you loved me, but it is “eternally” true no longer! Once, I think, you had your humanity, and could trust your senses well enough then. But you want to be like God, you want to be certain. Only God himself can be certain: we humans must just have faith! Faith comes and goes, and I have lost my faith now that Jean has been taken away from me. But at least faith and doubt are humble; they are not as arrogant as you!

Descartes — *(Looks at her for a moment, perplexed).* I do not believe I am arrogant, for I am humbled by the truths of the universe. Ambitious, perhaps, to want to discover them: but that is part of being human, that curiosity. That is why we were created, perhaps! What is the point of existing, if you do not seek the truth?

Kisa — What is the point of existing, if you do not have enough humanity left to grieve at the death of your own son! I do not believe we will ever understand each other, René. I will go and leave you to your arrogant abstractions.

Descartes	Where are you going?

Kisa	I do not know.

Descartes	Stay! You do not have to go back out into this terrible night! Wait till tomorrow, then we can bury the child and you can return to the town after that.

Kisa	No, I am going now, and taking my burden of griefs. I will leave you to your meditations.

Descartes	At least let me give you some money!

Kisa	Farewell. No, wait, I will give *you* something. A dog or a horse, you said. Something to meditate upon.

(Hands Descartes the dead baby)

This is your son. He is yours. Look after him well.

Descartes	But....

Kisa	Goodbye (*Exits swiftly)*

Variation 12: Hume

Mr. Hume causes a Riot by attacking Baby "Miracle"

At a crowded public meeting yesterday, Mr. David Hume, the notorious Scottish Philosopher often accused of atheism, made himself still more unpopular by his pronouncements upon the Hackney "Miracle Baby" case. As previously reported by this correspondent, Mrs. Gwendolen Kisa, of Hackney, claimed that her previously dead Baby had been brought back to life by a Miracle. According to her account, the Baby, having been pronounced dead by a Surgeon last month, was taken by Mrs Kisa to an Indian magician, the notorious "Bouddha of the East End", Mr Gow Tamma. Mr Tamma was then said to have brought the Baby back to life for the sum of three shillings and threepence. Mr Tamma and Mrs Kisa have been publicising this miracle all over London ever since, to the consternation of more educated and less credulous persons. Needless to say, Mr Tamma is now in great demand for everything from the curing of warts to bringing back one's dead grandmother. A group of Scientific Gentlemen evidently collaborated to sponsor a Public Meeting in response to this Quackery, and employed Mr Hume as a forceful speaker on the side of Reason.

In the meeting held yesterday, Mr. Hume ascended to the rostrum with an air of calm and immovable Rationality, though he was heckled from the beginning. He argued that we should not believe any such claims of Miracles as this one, for Miracles are against the Laws of Nature. The Laws of Nature, he claimed, are known only through the Senses, which, though imperfect, are our only source of True Knowledge. What the Senses normally tell us should be accepted as True, said Mr Hume, and reports of events which go against the Laws of Nature are more likely to be False than True.

In the case of the Kisa Baby, he argued that there are better reasons for believing that Mrs Kisa and Mr Tamma are lying (since they have much to gain by doing so), or mistaken (since neither are well-educated in the principles of modern science), than we have for thinking that this unlikely miraculous event is True. It is very likely that this important point was missed by many members of the audience, who booed and heckled at the instigation of Mrs Kisa and Mr Tamma.

At this point Mrs Kisa stood up to defend her reputation, arguing that Mr Tamma was well-known to have Miraculous Powers, and to understand the underlying forces of the Universe. He knew much more about "Laws of Nature", than Mr Hume did, she claimed. At this point Mr Tamma, who does not speak very good English, nodded and signed his Approval. Mrs Kisa went on to claim that all her Friends and Neighbours could vouch for her Honesty.

When the noise had at last died down, Mr Hume replied that he did not know by what mysterious means Mr Tamma gained his knowledge of the "Laws of Nature", but it could not be by the commonly approved and accepted method of the Senses. As for Mrs Kisa, Mr Hume said he did not know any of the details of her Reputation, but the Testimony of her Friends must be weighed against the whole contrary Testimony of Mankind that such Miracles do not occur.

At this point, the Rev. Holly, a clergyman from Hackney, stood up and attacked Mr Hume for his alleged Atheism, appealing to the miracles in the New Testament and asking whether Mr Hume also disbelieved in these. Mr Hume replied that Belief in the New Testament Miracles was a matter of Faith and could not be rationally justified.

At this point the meeting broke down in uproar, and Mr Hume was obliged to make a quick exit in fear of life and limb. The Present Writer must express agreement with Mr Hume over his strong arguments against the "Miracle Baby" and other dubious cases of this kind, but not, of course, with his casting doubt on the Miracles of the New Testament, which being found in Scripture are quite a different matter.

Variation 13: Kant

I used to be a good friend of Immanuel Kant's. In our youth we were students together at the university, and when he was a young tutor we used to play billiards together. Kant used to empty my pockets in the most civilised manner possible, simply by applying his skill, and I never had the heart to refuse to bet, knowing how useful he found the money. As we got older, I moved away to Berlin. Kant stayed in Königsberg, and our contact grew less frequent. Whenever I came back to Königsberg to visit friends and relatives, though, he always gave me a warm welcome. He would entertain me to dinner, always eager for news from the capital, where he had never been.

It was on one such occasion later in our lives, when I found myself asking Kant's moral advice. We had been out of touch for some time – at least two years – when I visited on this occasion, and as I met him again I realised how much I regretted this and valued contact with my upright friend. He was delighted to see me after such a long interval, and extremely hospitable, despite being much occupied with his work. He had recently published his first important book on ethics, his *Groundwork of the Metaphysics of Morals*, but I could never have the patience for reading such heavy stuff myself. I wanted his advice for a more practical reason, without lots of theory, and I had a sense that he might be able to help me. The problem was one that lay close to my heart, though, and at first I was not quite sure how to approach it.

“Do you really believe, my friend, that your moral philosophy can provide guidance to every man in every circumstance?” I asked, between mouthfuls of liver sausage.

“If it could not guide every man in every circumstance, it would not be a moral philosophy!” Kant replied. “No duty is moral if it is not universal. It must be incumbent on all, equally, without exception, if it is to be a moral duty. In my view that is the whole difference between moral duties and other kinds of duties. A moral duty is a universal duty, but a non-moral duty is one that only applies in some particular set of circumstances.”

“Then, as my situation is one where I would like to know my moral duty, I wonder if I could ask your advice about one particular case.”

“How could I refuse such advice to such an old friend! Go ahead, Walter.”

“It is about my wife.”

Kant’s eyes widened slightly in surprise, and I realised that I had never told him about my marriage. I remembered thinking of writing to him to let him know, but then feeling uncomfortable about doing so and doing something else instead.

“I don’t believe I have met the good lady,” said Kant. “And I don’t think you can have been long married, can you?

For when I saw you last, as far as I remember, there was no mention of marriage."

"We were married in Berlin last year. It is late in my life to give up being a bachelor, I know, but I had begun to see old age ahead, and believe that I would need a young wife to help me through it. Then I met Kisa, a very pretty and spirited young thing, who seemed quite happy to marry a dull old fellow like me. I was flattered by how eagerly she accepted my proposal, and we got married very quickly. But she's not much of a traveller –like yourself, Immanuel – so I've never brought her to Königsberg."

For a moment I almost fancied I saw a flicker of emotion in Kant's eyes, which I might have ascribed to a touch of envy, had I not known him better. I knew he would never marry, for I could never imagine what wife would be able to live with so much stern rectitude and precision, tempered though it often was with kindness. Nor would he ever allow thoughts of female company to distract him from the discipline of his work.

"Still, you have made the marriage now, so presumably it is not your marriage that you wish to ask my advice about?"

"Indeed not. There is more to tell. Very soon after we were married, Kisa fell pregnant, and earlier this year a baby was born: a handsome boy in good health."

“I had no idea you were a father as well. My congratulations!”

“I’m afraid congratulations are now no longer appropriate. Two weeks ago the baby died, very suddenly and mysteriously.”

“I’m very sorry to hear that.”

“The trouble is, that when I left Berlin two days ago, Kisa had still not got over this. She has been absolutely destroyed by the death. I had to leave because I could not bear to be in the house with her any longer. She still carries the corpse of the baby around with her, and will not let it go.”

“Good heavens! After two weeks!”

“The flesh has been rotting, and the corpse has begun to stink, but she still carries it around with her and speaks to it, and tries to feed it from her breast. She will not listen to any reason, and when I try to take the baby away she becomes absolutely savage and clings onto it fiercely.” The pain of recalling all this, so recent, began to rise to my throat, and I had to cover my face with my hands. “I’m sorry.” When I looked up again, Kant was looking directly at me with eyes full of compassion.

“It sounds like madness, Walter. Have you seen a physician?”

"Yes, several. They all said that the baby should be taken from her forcibly, and she should be taken to a hospital for the insane. But I cannot bear to do it, for I feel that it is my fault that she is like this, that I brought her to this by marrying her."

"Come, come! How could it be your fault?"

"If I had not married her so young, she would not have had to face this. I feel that I married her for my comfort, not hers, and somehow this has been my punishment."

"No, Walter, this is irrational. You cannot be to blame." Kant got up and began to pace the room, somewhat stiffly, leaving his potatoes uneaten. "For who would blame any man for acting as you did? You did not marry her against her will, but she freely entered into the contract. You have not treated her as a means to an end."

"I don't think you understand. Before we were married, yes, she was free enough: free as a bird that willingly flies into its cage, to have the door shut on it. But after we were married, when she became pregnant, she began to change."

"In what way?"

"She began to lose interest in things. She did not sleep. She became listless. When I asked her what was the matter, she would not tell me. But looking back at it now, I believe she felt trapped."

"But she did not tell you so?"

"No. She would never admit it. Then when her baby was born, suddenly she was so happy again, she was so devoted to it. She had a new interest in life. I began to think that what she had been through was just a phase women go through after marriage, and that now she was a mother we would all be happy. And so it seemed – until the baby died."

"I see. Well, perhaps she did feel trapped. But I still do not think you are to blame at all. When we enter a contract like marriage, freely, we are using our practical reason. It is our responsibility to consider such a step carefully, and to ensure that we are acting in accordance with duty, not simply in accordance with desire. If we act rashly in making such a contract, nevertheless we are responsible for our step and should act in accordance with our commitments. As long as she was an adult in possession of her reason, it was her responsibility to act autonomously in deciding whether to marry you. So you have not abused her in any way. Your conscience should be clear, Walter."

I nodded, and realised that I felt relieved. With such an upright man before me, I could believe what he said, and feel more fully absolved than any Christian priest could have made me. "But Immanuel," I went on, "It is not just that I feel guilty. I cannot bear to send her to an asylum. I do not know what to do next."

Kant paused in his pacing. "What to do next? Hm. Well, you asked me about my moral philosophy. This is my moral philosophy: act according to that maxim which you can will to be a universal law. So, look at yourself and your situation. Try to leave your feelings behind and use reason alone, for feelings will not lead you to do your duty. Think what you would wish every man in your situation to do, what principle you would wish him to follow."

"I do not know."

"Think of the possible courses of action before you. What could you do?"

"I could take the baby away from her by force and bury it, and send her to the hospital."

"And if you did that, what principle would you be following?"

"I do not understand." I became confused.

"What would you be trying to do? What would be the intention behind that action if you were to do it?"

"I would be trying to help her, and release her from suffering; and myself too, I suppose."

"And would you not want every man to act in that way in similar circumstances?"

"Yes, I suppose so."

"Then you would be following a universal maxim. You would be doing your duty. I believe that you should follow what your reasoning tells you to do, not your feelings of guilt. In any case, what else could you do? What alternative course of action is there?"

"I could leave her to carry on like this – with this mad pretence."

"And if you did that, what maxim would you be following?"

I paused, confused again. "I'm not sure."

"Then let me tell you, Walter. You would be indulging your irrational feelings of guilt. If you would not want every man in your circumstance to indulge his irrational feelings of guilt, then do not act in that way."

I swallowed. "Yes, I think I see. It is hard, but I think you have given me the right advice. Indeed, you have told me what I ought to have known for myself."

"It is not just your duty to yourself that is involved, Walter; it is your duty to her. You are bound to her by a contract for the rest of your days. It is your duty to do what will be best for her."

"Yes, yes, I see. I think I have to go. Yes, I must get the next stagecoach back to Berlin, without delay. Thank you, Immanuel: I am immensely indebted to you for what you have made clear to me this evening." I looked into his eyes and saw only stern friendship. "I don't know why I had to come as far as Königsberg to start thinking straight, but I am grateful to you nevertheless. I will write and let you know the issue of this business."

Leaving my long-neglected liver sausage half-eaten, I rushed from the room.

Variation 14: Bentham

Jeremy Bentham to James Mill, esquire

Dear James,

In your last letter you ask me a vexing question which it has been much my trouble to try to answer, though I think I have it now. You ask me whether it is truly for the greatest good of the greatest number that everyone should judge by utilitarian principles, given that some will not judge them justly. At first I found this question in your letter, but put it by for a while upon more pressing business. However, a most vexing incident recently has made me once more conscious of it, and meant I most instantly required a solution of it. I will explain the circumstance.

There is a young man, the son of my neighbour, Sir William Hunt, who is also called William and has always been a most credulous youth. He was much struck with the doctrines of utilitarianism when listening to me talking to Sir William as a boy, and would often ask me about them. When he got a bit older though, he started to go into the city and do the things that young gentlemen do, in company with his friends. Sometimes his father wouldn't see him for days on end, but he didn't seem too concerned.

Then one day, when I called upon Sir William upon some other business, I found him very downcast. He explained that he was very disappointed in young William, who had always been so much his father's favourite, and so eager about utilitarianism. He had just heard some very disappointing news about him (and here he begged my secrecy), that he had got a wench with child! All this sporting in London had clearly done him no good, and his dubious friends no better. I expressed my disapprobation of his behaviour.

But the news got worse as the months went by. It seemed that the girl was not just some serving maid, but come from quite a respectable family, though fallen on hard times and not well-off. Her parents, on hearing the news, threw her out of the house and would have nothing more to do with her. Sir William insisted that his son find her a place to live, and paid for it from his own expenses, to save her from the workhouse. All this bad news came to me in instalments from Sir William, who badly needed a confidant. I was very happy to relieve him and sympathise, but it never occurred to me at this time that the business would come to more closely concern myself.

Then, last week, I heard that the baby had been born: a sickly and fretful baby. Sir William continued to ensure that the girl was quietly taken care of, and it seemed that young William was remorseful and wanted to marry her, but Sir William would not hear of him throwing away his prospects and his reputation in such a way.

Then just yesterday, to my astonishment, I received a call from young William. He came in with a furtive, hunted expression and said immediately, “Mr Bentham, please, I need your help. You must hide me!”

“Hide you? Whatever for? And who from? If this is some game….”

“No, no,” he insisted, “I am in earnest. The constables are looking for me. I have done no wrong, but I have broken the law. I know you will help me, for I have only followed the principles you always taught.”

At this point a foreboding of the young man’s real naïveté and its effects struck me, but I still pretended mere astonishment. “Followed the principles I always taught? But the constables are after you? What have you done?”

“I killed the baby, Kisa’s baby. I thought she would be pleased, but she didn’t understand at all. She went and told the constables. It was all to produce the greatest happiness of the greatest number, you see. I was unhappy, Kisa was unhappy, the baby was unhappy, my father was unhappy, her father was unhappy. What was the life of a sickly child, like to die anyway, compared to all that unhappiness it was causing? I was sure I was doing the right thing.” He went on like this at some length, justifying himself in the most ludicrous fashion imaginable, until I interrupted him.

“You fool!” I cried, “You absolute fool! I never taught you this! Can’t you see that if the state were to bring in a law for the killing of sickly and illegitimate infants, that would be one thing, but to take it into your own hands another!

Dear God! Now you are a murderer and may be hanged! If it were left to the judgement of every man who begets a bastard that he might kill it, where would the country be! Full of infanticides and bloody babes! Utilitarianism does not override the law, but bids you follow the law for the greatest happiness of all, and where it wants alteration argue your case in parliament! If you break the law you must meet its penalties. You will go to the scaffold!"

The boy looked absolutely terrified. His whole security had collapsed in a moment, for he seemed to have absolutely believed that I would support him in a secret moral crusade against the law. At length he cried, "Please, help me! I have been such a fool. I felt it was wrong when I plunged in the knife, but I made myself do it for the greater good. Please help me!"

"I will not defend you." I replied, "If you give your naïve utilitarian justification as defence, you will be laughed out of court." Then it occurred to me that utilitarianism would also become the laughingstock of London, and many good purposes we have for reform, which would indeed really bring greater happiness, would be set back for many years. "I have a good mind to let you hang for this" I said, not quite truly, "but I will help you as much as I can for your father's sake. Go and hide in the cellar for now: if the constables call I don't think they will search this house when I give my word falsely, breaking the law myself for your sake. I will try to make arrangements to get you abroad, and I will tell Sir William what has passed secretly after you are gone, but no-one else. You must make a new life for yourself, giving up all expectation of inheritance, all familiar habits, and count yourself lucky to be alive. Go!"

So, having explained the circumstances, it is now that I must ask your help, dear James. Please could you use your position at the East India Company to find him a secret passage out of London on a ship? It does not matter where. A ship bound for India might drop him en route, perhaps in Lisbon, with little trouble, I think. I will undertake to get him to the docks in a closed carriage, if you will arrange a discreet passage on board ship. As soon as possible, for he cannot stay hiding in my cellar for ever, and I have already put off two constables and Sir William.

But my tale is not yet done, for it is not only the boy that had to be considered if the reputation of utilitarianism is to be saved. I also had to see the girl and ensure her silence. I travelled in haste to the lodgings I knew had been found for her by Thames Street, and found to my relief that she had told no-one else but the constables. My relief on this score, however, was tempered by distress at the distracted state I found her in, still holding the dead baby. At first I started to explain to her why William had done the deed, why I was also concerned, and why it was important to maintain silence, but I soon realised this was useless, for she was not taking in my words. All I could get out of her was that she loved the baby, that William was evil, but that she felt she had done the killing too.

“How can you have done it?” I asked, “Wasn’t it William who killed the child?”

“But I was complaining!” She cried, “When really the baby was the best thing that ever happened to me, the greatest thing I ever loved! It was me who did it really!”

Suddenly I was struck by another thought, and no longer attempted to remove this idea from her mind. Her confusion might do what her clarity could not.

I then did the hardest thing I have ever done, though with mature consideration and, I think, a clear conscience. I went and told the constable that it was my regrettable duty to inform him that, on talking to Miss Kisa in relation to the legal aspects of the case, she had herself confessed to killing the baby, meaning that her accusation against young Mr William Hunt must be false. I may have to commit perjury in court before all this is finished, but in a good cause. If you wonder at me, James, think of all the thousands, nay millions, who will benefit from the utilitarian reforms we are proposing. What is the life of a girl compared to all that unhappiness relieved?

I then immediately returned home, so have not yet been informed whether Miss Kisa has been arrested, or how that case is progressing. You may think that if it succeeds, then young William can be saved from his exile. I would not agree with this line of thinking, for to remove all risk he must not be in the country when this case goes to court, and there is also a risk that the case may fail because her testimony will be so inconsistent. Perhaps he can return after a few years when it has all blown over. I think we can rely upon Sir William's discretion particularly in that case, and of course I know I can rely absolutely on yours.

I think that I now probably no longer need to answer the question you posed in your last letter. Certainly those who do not judge justly should not attempt to judge by utilitarian principles. Heaven save utilitarianism from those who do not judge it justly! We must make a stronger point from now on, I believe, of stating that utilitarianism is a principle for legislators, not for personal conduct. For personal conduct we should follow law and common morality, the following of which is in general for the greatest happiness of the greatest number, and thus indirectly supported by our principles.

Yours etc.
Jeremy Bentham

The Moderns

Variation 15: Marx

Scene: A shabby, overcrowded house in Victorian London, full of the cries of young children who are running around the floor. Jenny Marx is trying to mend worn-out clothes, but is being constantly interrupted by the children. Karl Marx is sitting in a corner trying to read a weighty book, but frequently pulls out his watch with exclamations like "What can be the problem!", and "Where is he?" At length, Friedrich Engels stumbles through the door.

Engels — Ah, good-day Karl, and good-day Mrs Marx, I am so sorry to be so late. I know I said I'd be here at midday, but I was most unexpectedly delayed in Manchester, and had to catch a later train. However, I have got the money I know you need so urgently. (*Pulls out a sheaf of banknotes and hands them to Karl).*

J.Marx — Gott sei Dank! I don't know how we'd manage without you, Mr Engels. We are so grateful to you. The landlord might have thrown us out by the end of the week without you.

K.Marx — Don't thank God, Jenny, thank the material conditions of Friedrich's factory. And Friedrich isn't really doing it just for us, you know, but so that my work can continue. One day, all this will be unnecessary. People won't have to struggle to pay the rent, because there will be no rent. The means of sustenance will be freely given one to another without the need for money. People will be able to contribute to society in whatever way they want and will work freely, because there will be no more alienation and class-struggle. However, in the meantime, of course we need your help to promote the proletarian revolution, and I am very grateful for it, Friedrich.

Engels — Don't mention it. As you say, it's all for the great cause.

K.Marx — So what happened in Manchester to delay you so much?

Engels — It's rather a long story. Though quite an interesting story, I think.

K.Marx — Then sit down and tell it! (*brushes children's playthings off a chair and offers it to Engels*). Jenny, get the man some tea if we have some!

J.Marx I'm afraid we have none. There has been no money for tea. Even bread for the last few days has been on the baker's credit, and he is getting impatient. We do not even have fuel for the stove, though thankfully it is not too cold at present. I've been at my wit's end thinking how to feed the children.

K.Marx Then leave your sewing and go out and buy tea, milk, and fuel! We have a guest in our humble home. (*Hands Jenny one of the notes Engels has just given him, and she leaves*).(*Turns to Engels*) So, what's the story?

Engels It concerns one of my female workers at the mill, just an ordinary hand, but with an odd name for an Englishwoman – Kisa, she is called.

K.Marx How did she get a name as odd as that?

Engels I have no idea, and she has never offered me any explanation. Her parents are hands too, and perhaps having so little freedom in their lives leads them to exercise it as much as they can in other ways, like giving children fanciful names. You can imagine how the men make fun of her and call her "Kisser", begging her for a kiss, though she's not the type to offer kisses to all comers.

K.Marx — I'm glad to hear it, but what does this strangely-named hand have to do with your being delayed this morning?

Engels — Well, I checked in at the mill very early this morning before leaving for the railway station, with the intention of just giving a few last-minute instructions to the foremen before the day began. The workers were just clattering through the streets in the dim light of dawn. However, when I got to my office, a most alarming and unexpected sight met my eyes! (*hesitates*).

K.Marx — Go on then, what was it?

Engels — Kisa was standing there in the most frantic state, holding a dead baby. The babies of hands dying is common enough, but I think this was her first, and she seemed to have gone insane. She said *I* was to blame for it! Can you imagine!

K.Marx — How could you possibly be to blame? (*pauses*) Unless it was an indiscretion of yours, Friedrich? You haven't been exercising *droit de seigneur* over your factory hands, have you?

Engels — Good heavens, no! How could you think such a thing, Karl?

K.Marx — Well, it's all part of the material oppression of the proletariat, you know: not just money, property and power, but special favours from the wenches as well. You might as well make the most of it while it lasts. But never mind: pray don't take offence and do continue.

Engels — Well, I have rarely been so insulted! In front of your children too!

K.Marx — I do apologise. I didn't mean it in a personal way. You mustn't mistake my remarks on the nature of class oppression in general for personal ones. And the children are all too young to understand.

Engels — (*Reluctantly soothed)* Well, to return to my story. Kisa's ranting that I was to blame was nothing to do with any question of paternity, make no mistake. Instead, it was about her poverty and conditions of life, that she said were to blame for her baby's death. She said they were so poor, and food prices so high, that she was forced to buy bad grain that made her and all her family ill. The whole family was missing from work so long that they depended on the charity of neighbours to survive, and the neighbours could not give much because they were hard put to it themselves. In the end, with the starvation and the illness, her milk dried up, with the baby not yet weaned. There was no other woman who could serve as wet-nurse and no money for cow's milk, and the baby just died of starvation. If I paid the hands decent wages, or gave them sick-pay, she said, the baby would still be alive.

K.Marx — This doesn't sound like insane rantings to me. It sounds like a truthful picture of the oppression of the proletariat.

Engels — It is true that her rantings had reason in them. I would easily have sent her away at once so I would not be delayed, but I was struck by the fact that, although she was in an extreme state of agitated grief, and her account of how the baby had died came out gradually, and in a much less coherent way than my summary, it did have sense in it.

K.Marx — But I hope you did not agree that you were at fault?

Engels — Oh no, of course not. I told her that it was the capitalist system that was responsible for her situation and for the death of her baby. I told her that I had every sympathy, but that if I gave the hands higher wages or gave them sick-pay, I would not be able to compete in the capitalist economic system. However, I urged her to look forward to the future day when the proletarian revolution would occur, and the workers would right the oppression of capitalism.

K.Marx — Did she understand?

Engels — I think so, in the end, though it took a long time to get across in her half-starved and agitated state. She kept thrusting the dead baby in my face and saying "Ne'er mind the capi'list eeknomic sys'em, what about this 'ere dead babby?". It took a long while to calm her enough to understand what I was saying, but she is not a stupid woman, even though uneducated. I thought it was important to make the effort, because here was a chance to communicate the scientific truth of the matter to a member of the proletariat. I think she understood in the end, but she did not accept what I was saying.

K.Marx — Did she raise any rational objections, or did she just reject your case because of her nervous state?

Engels — More rational objections than you might expect. Indeed, they have been giving me pause for thought whilst I was riding in the train hither.

K.Marx — Really? A mill-hand shaking your scientific principles?

Engels — She did not have abstract principles to match mine, there is no fear there. No, rather than offer opposing principles, she just made me sharply aware of the immediate life and experience of the proletariat. For her, my scientific explanation of future proletarian revolution could never be anything other than an excuse to avoid my responsibility for bettering their conditions. Nothing I could say about the material conditions made any difference to that.

K.Marx — Ach! But you know, Friedrich, it is all part of the intellectual superstructure that enables the oppressive system. The illusion of freewill, the illusion of responsibility. How can we be to blame for anything, when we are all the result of material conditions?

Engels — Yes, I know that, but.... Well, take just now when I gave you the money and you thanked me, even though it was all for the great work. Why did you thank me if I was neither responsible for earning the money nor even for giving it to you?

K.Marx — We have talked about all this before, don't you remember? My thanks are themselves a result of the material conditions. We have to observe the social mechanisms of the society that we live in. But in the Communist

Society, there will be no need for gratitude because there will be no need for charity. Those who have enough do not have to express thanks to their benefactors any more. Gratitude is a part of bourgeois morality, as is responsibility and freewill. We have to play by those rules and pretend to live by those illusions for now, that's all.

Engels (*Sighs*) Yes, I understand. But it is hard sometimes. Sometimes I feel that I might just be peddling more lies and fantasies that support the power of the bourgeoisie, just like the Church does.

K.Marx I have never known you like this before, Friedrich. You must put aside these doubts that this woman has sown in you. We cannot possibly be peddling more lies and fantasies, because we have scientific analysis on our side! I must tell you more about how my work has been progressing, because I am going to produce a definitive scientific account of capitalism and its superstructure! Never fear: once our work becomes more widely known and understood, people will flock to us!

Engels Perhaps you are right. It is just not so easy being a communist mill-owner, you know.

(Jenny Marx re-enters, loaded with faggots, tea and milk)

J.Marx Here we are! It will still take a while to light the stove, I'm afraid, but tea is on its way. All while you gentlemen sit around talking! A woman's labours are never done! What is the communist revolution going to do for women, that's what I've often asked Mr Marx, but I never get a straight answer....

Variation 16: Schopenhauer

The air was balmy, with the lightest of sea-breezes, and the light clear, as the sun sank over the Pacific. Art had the beach to himself, and was in a spacious, reflective mood. He gazed at the tangerine hues of the setting sun, and wondered if he could induce one of those experiences Schopenhauer talked about, where the Will is silenced for a short time, and one achieves a blissful aesthetic sense of being lifted beyond the cares of the earth. Straining at the setting sun, he tried to let himself slide into a sense of ecstasy. But it was no good, it didn't quite work. Perhaps it was the dope he'd had yesterday interfering, he thought.

His contemplation was interrupted by Kisa running down from the beachside holiday home where they were staying, borrowed from Art's parents. She was calling for him and looked anxious. He was rather disinclined to meet such anxiety: he really wasn't feeling anxious right now, and didn't want his good mood interrupted. So instead of going to meet Kisa, he just contemplated the pleasing lines of her body, in bikini top and beach wrap, and long flowing black hair, as she ran across the beach. He thought what a lovely girl she was, and how lucky he had been to find her. Shame about the baby though – he really hadn't wanted a baby so soon, but accidents do happen.

"Art, Art, come quickly! Don't just stand there!"

“What’s the trouble?”

“It’s the baby! I’m worried about the baby! He’s not breathing properly. Come and see!”

“I expect he’s fine,” said Art, but nevertheless reluctantly began to follow her back to the holiday home. The sleeping baby did seem to be breathing in a slightly irregular way, but he really couldn’t imagine it was anything to worry about.

“I want to call the physician.”

“Nah. It’s really nothing to worry about. I expect it’s just normal baby stuff. You really shouldn’t worry so much about things, Kisa. Just be cool!”

Since she had first met him at the Freshers’ Prom at Berkeley last year, Kisa had had a weakness for Art’s cool. It met some sort of need for security in her. The academic fight to get to Berkeley, and before that her parents’ divorce, together with a childhood in transition between India and California, had all exaggerated her tendency towards anxiety. It was so good just to believe his assurance that everything would be all right, so she could sometimes let go of that constant flutter in her head when in his arms. The fact that he was a philosophy major also sometimes made her feel he had unlocked the secrets of the universe, or something like that. Her own specialisation in business, chosen out of anxiety for her future career prospects, had no such allure.

So, when she believed Art's reassurances, she was following her habit. She did so not because he had always been proved right (as on the night he had persuaded her to have sex without contraception on the grounds that "it would be all right", making her pregnant in her second year at college); rather she believed him because it made her feel better to do so. Relief began to flood into her mind the moment she began to dismiss the worry, on Art's authority.

"Why don't you come out onto the beach with me, and see the sunset while the baby's still asleep? Leave the door open, then we'll hear him if he wakes up."

They both stood and contemplated the sun, now just a red sliver over the horizon, with gentle waves before them tinged with pink.

"I've been thinking about Schopenhauer," said Art, "and the things he said about contemplative experiences."

"Contemplative experiences? Do they come up in philosophy too? I thought they were a religious thing."

"They certainly do in Schopenhauer. Schopenhauer is the only philosopher who really understands the experience of artists. He spends a lot of time with the arts – going to plays, concerts, that kind of thing. A lot of other philosophers today are really sort of second-hand scientists. They have such a dry way of looking at the universe and take away all the magic. You know how much my father likes the arts, and he likes Schopenhauer too: that's why he called me Arthur, you know."

"Really? You never told me that. So that was Schopenhauer's first name?"

"Yep. Arthur Schopenhauer."

"But what's this about contemplative experiences?"

"Schopenhauer thought we are all part of the Will, the force that goes through everything and drives everyone through their desires, remember that?" Kisa nodded. "But he also thought that sometimes we can get free of the Will, we can get beyond all this frantic wanting this or that for a few moments, and achieve a blissful peace. That's probably what artists experience at their most inspired."

"Ah, I could really do with some blissful peace getting beyond all the frantic cares, Art. What with all the college papers, trying to fit everything else in my schedule around the baby, sleepless nights, and my Mom's disapproval. It's really nice being here with you, Art. I'm so glad your parents could lend us this house."

They turned to each other and kissed as the sun finally fell below the horizon. They lingered in each other's arms and then started strolling hand-in-hand by the waves.

But Art's mind still kept recurring to Schopenhauer. "Schopenhauer really is the most cool philosopher. He thought the very best, most admirable people were the ascetics, like saints who are above all pleasure and pain. They defy the Will. It doesn't matter to them what happens, whatever deaths or illnesses occur, it just washes over them, because reacting to all that is just how we're driven by the Will. Just imagine what it would be like to be as free as that, Kisa! It wouldn't matter what grades we got in our term papers, or if there was some little thing wrong with the baby. No worries! We could just live in eternal tranquillity."

Kisa's reason finally began to rebel a little at this. "That sounds great in theory, Art, but not much good in practice. If we never worried about anything, then surely we'd never do anything. Before long we would starve to death!"

"What would that matter? It's only the tyranny of the Will that makes us so concerned about continuing to live. Death is the great unknown beyond the self, beyond the world, beyond our experience. But if we conquer the Will – almost impossible because we are formed by it and run by it, like everything else on earth – but if we conquer the Will we are free from all fears of pain or death."

"But if you conquered the Will you wouldn't want me, would you?"

Art grinned, "You're right, it is almost impossible to conquer the Will, especially where you are concerned."

They chased each other back to the beach house in the gathering darkness, and ended up making love on the sofa. Then, as the baby still did not stir, they made a pleasant supper *á deux*.

* * * * * * * * *

Kisa had an uneasy night. Unconsciously she expected the baby to wake her, but it did not stir, so though she did not wake up fully during the night she had slept an anxious sleep. She dreamt that the Will was coming to take her baby, as a great black cloud of terror. She tried to wake Art to make it go away, but Art just said "No worries. It's just a baby thing." The Will came nearer and nearer, and was about to take her baby from her, when she woke up with a start. It was dawn, she was drenched with sweat, and Art was sleeping peacefully beside her.

She realised that the baby must have been asleep for about 10 hours without a feed. He never slept for that long! She sprang to the cot, and suddenly all her fears were icily confirmed. The baby was stiff and cold and showed no signs of life.

In a moment of extreme shock, not only her assurance about the baby but also all her trust in Art evaporated. "Art! Art! Wake up!" She tried to say, cradling the little body, but it only came out as a half-audible croak. She made a tremendous effort and this time shouted "Art! Art! Wake up!"

Art rolled over and looked at the clock. "Mm Kisa, it's only four in the morning. Can't you feed the baby without disturbing me? I know it's hard getting up in the night, but there's no need to be a dog in the manger you know."

Kisa could not speak, but eventually Art realised there was something wrong. He touched the baby and gasped just one word, "Cold!"

This word somehow broke the barrier that was holding Kisa's speech, and rage tumbled out.

"Cold! She's dead! Thanks to you and your fucking cool! I knew he wasn't right and then you said 'it's just a baby thing' and went on about Schopenhauer. As though you knew! We should have called a physician! He could be alive now and He's gone, d'you understand, gone! All because of your bloody philosophy!"

Art sat on the bed for a few moments in silence, then at length said gently "But Kisa, you could see it differently. Remember what we were saying last night?"

Kisa did not reply.

"He's gone beyond the Will, beyond pleasure and pain, beyond the troubles of this world. He is free. It is not our doing: whatever you say I don't think I am responsible for his death. But when the universe is such a difficult place, he may be better off being free of it."

Kisa glowered and then abruptly got up, still holding the dead baby. "Art, I never want to see you again. Keep your bloody Schopenhauer to yourself. I'm going to my Mom's right now and taking the baby."

Art never ceased to protest as she pulled on her clothes, and followed her to the front door, where she laid the baby's body on the front seat of her car. "Goodbye Art" she snapped, and started the engine. In moments he was left standing alone on the doorstep in the chill early morning.

Variation 17: Sartre and De Beauvoir

Sartre and De Beauvoir sometimes liked to linger over their early morning coffee and Gauloise, before they turned to their separate desks and separate philosophical inspirations.

This morning De Beauvoir looked disturbed and restless. She had had a disturbing dream which she was keen to tell Sartre about.

“I had a dream of a woman with a dead baby.” She told him. “She railed and screamed. She was a fury against the injustice of the baby’s death. She accused God, she accused patriarchy. Why did it have to be taken away so soon, when her instincts to nurture it were so strong? Why did her suffering matter so little to men, that they wanted to dismiss it or explain it away with their patriarchal God, when here was the very dead baby in her arms? Why do women have to suffer like this, made so vulnerable to the loss of one little life? Why is this fate so different from men, who never love another being like this and thus cannot suffer so?”

“Did you speak to her in the dream?”

“No, I was silent. There were men who offered many different answers that she angrily rejected: a priest, a psychologist, a philosopher. But I had no answers so I did not offer any. I simply wondered at her and felt with her fury.”

"So you were angry too?"

"Not exactly. I understood her anger. It pierced me to my heart, and seemed to stand for the anger of all women, but I also looked on it calmly and in an almost puzzled way. I am still puzzled by the dream."

"Well, you can easily guess what Monsieur Freud might say about it."

"A lot of time you have for Monsieur Freud! You don't even believe in the unconscious! Well, what do you think he would say then?"

"That the dream represented your own frustrated desire for a child, perhaps, or maybe a complex about your father which has dramatically erupted in the form of an attack on men in general."

"You don't believe that, I take it! No, I would not blame the dream on any external or physiological cause. It is part of my own mind."

"Indeed, that is much more my way of seeing things. We cannot rid ourselves of responsibility for our dream selves without bad faith. But that may mean that in a sense the woman is you. The woman reflects your own choices in some way."

At this point De Beauvoir paused for a few moments, stubbing her Gauloise and staring into space. At length she went on, “Yes, I believe the woman stands for my own rage against the constraint of women. While men have been expected to choose their own lives, the lives of women have only been those of shadows in the wake of men’s choices. The dead child is not any real or desired infant, but all the authentic lives that might have been, if they had not been killed by patriarchy. The child stands for all of women’s frustrated hopes throughout the centuries.”

“Isn’t that putting it rather too grandly? Isn’t it about *your* hopes? If you depersonalise it too much there’s a danger that you will lose the authenticity of your acknowledgement of it as yours.”

“It is my rage. I don’t pretend that all women are enraged. But nevertheless it is my rage about the status of all women. Think, Jean-Paul, of the “answers” she would have had in the past! That it is the will of God; that the child is in heaven; that it is not for a mere woman to question what has been ordained; that women have over-emotional reactions; or that she is “hysterical”, as only those with wombs can be! Through the ages she will only have been given one answer after another, all keeping her in her place, just calming her down so she can go away and have more children as society demands. I feel for all those women who have railed in vain.”

“I am not so sure that it is only women who have suffered when the only answers to their questions were in bad faith.” Sartre replied, “Men, too, suffer when their children die, and men also have many other projects that have 'died', burnt up by the dogmas of the age. I think your rage ought to extend beyond women."

"So it does. But my rage is specially for women. Their fate has been different because their facticity is different. They have a tenderness for their own child that a man can never have, and then when it is taken away, the power of the lies they are told to explain their loss is all the greater for their vulnerability. All suffer from bad faith, but the sorrow is all the greater for those who were more vulnerable to start with."

"Like men, though, such women are not just the victims of others' bad faith. They choose to believe what they are told."

"Yes, but can't you see the reason? They cannot accept their loss. They so much want their baby to be brought back to life that they will cling to anything that gives hope. The choice they are making is a choice to carry on hoping rather than to accept death and finality."

"But this is a false choice, surely? Better to be authentic and face the truth that death is the end."

"That is a man's answer! Yes, I agree it is in the end. But women's facticity is different. They have so much more to bear at moments such as the death of their child. It may be that accepting the reassuring lies is better than falling into despair or alienation. They may be better choosing them sometimes who could not choose to reject them."

Sartre nodded. “Yes, I can see what you are driving at. Our choices depend on our facticity, and we cannot blame those who made the most authentic choice available to them in the past. Nevertheless there will have been a few, women as well as men, who still questioned that facticity, and showed that everyone’s freedom went further than that. Just a few of those women with dead children in the past will not have accepted the answers, and will have railed on to the open heavens. Perhaps one could say that they just chose rage instead.”

De Beauvoir sprang up at this. “That is what I choose! And now I am going to commit my rage to writing.” She stood up and went out.

Sartre, however, stayed seated, and lit himself another contemplative Gauloise.

Variation 18: Jung

When I went to see Dr Jung, it was a bright and breezy afternoon, and the clouds were chasing each other over the Zürichsee. I took the train to Böllingen and then walked through the well-ordered streets to his house by the lake.

He greeted me with intensity. "I'm glad of the opportunity to see you separately from your daughter," he said, "Perhaps I can make you better acquainted with the underlying nature of the case."

I was ushered into his study, surrounded with books and carvings, and with pictures of mandalas framed on the walls.

"First, I'd like to express my gratitude to you, Doctor." I said, "I know you will see my daughter again, and her treatment is not yet complete, but she is so much better already. It seemed miraculous, when she came back so much calmer, and gave up the baby to be buried."

"Yes, I feared at first from her way of behaving that she might be psychotic and have to be hospitalised, but she responded to analysis very quickly. I think that is because her extreme grief was never wholly compulsive or unconscious in motivation. She had reason for it, and her bewilderment in the face of death only mirrors that which many of us encounter."

“But what did you do, Doctor, that made such a difference? You know how she came here believing that you could bring her baby back to life – yet after one session with you she was able to accept that it was dead!”

“Well, in a sense it is true you know – I can bring her baby back to life! But do not misunderstand me - in a psychological sense only. What I sought to do was to bring back to life the energies of her psyche that were focused on the baby. When the baby is alive it is natural for a mother to focus a huge amount of energy on it. It is when those energies cannot shift through a normal grieving process that there is something wrong.

“The first thing I had to do was to explain to her that the ‘baby’ she was so attached to was part of her own psyche. What she was actually grieving about was a baby-shaped space which was symbolised, or fetishised, by the baby’s body. This came to her as an entirely new recognition, but she is an intelligent girl and grasped it quickly. Once she could understand the object of her grief as internal, we could remove the external focus of it in the form of the body.

“But this is not enough by itself. A transfer from an outward to an inward process in no way ensures an appropriate process of grief by itself. Grief is adjustment to the new state of affairs. But when I saw her she seemed less subject to grief than to impotent rage. She wanted to blame the whole world rather than recognise the grief as hers. However, I think not really recognising the baby as dead, and carrying it round with her, enabled that rage to continue without progressing into grief. What I am concerned about is that a process of grief does begin. When it has occurred, then her energies can form relationships with other archetypes, not just the child. That is the main reason why I think it important to see your daughter again."

"What you say makes so much sense." I replied, "And I think she had begun to grieve even when she left you, because she was so much calmer. She has started to talk about the baby and look at photographs, rather than blaming us or blaming the world for what happened."

"That is good. However, the baby will only truly have been brought back to life again when she is able to engage in other occupations and develop other goals and sources of meaning. I will see her again as arranged next week. Meanwhile perhaps you could ask her to pay attention to her dreams and to try to keep a note of them."

"I will. Thank you, Herr Doktor."

On the way out of his study, I noticed an icon of the Virgin and Child hanging on the wall. For a single moment, the Child seemed dead and the Virgin to be raining tears upon it, but then I looked again and they resumed their stiff, iconic life.

Coda

Even the nights of an Indian winter can be cool, and Kisa woke up feeling stiff in the dawn light, as though the cold had reached into her bones. Many of her younger sisters were already meditating, but the elderly nun needed a bit more time to get up. Looking up at the straw roof, she suddenly remembered what she had been dreaming about – that baby, her baby, that had died so many years ago, on the same day that she had met the Buddha and become his disciple. She had not thought of that baby for many years, but suddenly she was conscious of many others, leaping within her, that might have been.

She told herself that she was engaging in vain regrets. After nearly fifty years as a nun, barren and wrinkled as she was, was this really the time to start worrying about the other children she had never had? No, she had devoted herself to the spiritual life, and that ought to be enough. Rising, she went to join her sisters in meditation and tried to put these thoughts aside.

After her alms-round, however, she decided that it was time that she should see the Buddha again. He was getting old too. Perhaps this would be a goodbye visit for both of them. She had something she wanted to ask him. As the Buddha constantly moved from place to place, she had to enquire as to his whereabouts. Fortunately, it turned out that he was in a village not more than five miles distant. Taking a younger sister with her, she began the walk, but found it quite enough of a distance to tax her. "I am getting old" she told her friend. "This body is becoming like a broken-down cart horse. I will not be able to go on too much longer."

However, she made it to the village where the Buddha was found, and the Buddha seemed to be glad to see her, though hardly able to disguise some of the pain he was feeling from bodily infirmity.

"Welcome, Kisa Gotami." He said, "Now we meet once more in the evening of our lives. My heart tells me that this will be the last time, and that neither of us has much longer to live."

"That may well be." Kisa replied. "I have come to see you, Master, because I have one more thing to ask before the end."

"What do you wish to ask?"

"On the day when I became your disciple, you told me that you taught the path to end all suffering. Yet I have been following that path for fifty years, and I am suffering still. What is more, I perceive that even you yourself are suffering, through the many infirmities, the aches and pains of age, just as I am. To follow this path, I put aside the joy of further children, which might have replaced the one I lost on the day I met you. Yet the promise of this path does not seem to have been fulfilled. Why are we still suffering?"

"I did indeed teach the path to end all suffering. But that does not mean that following that path will lead to the end of all suffering in this life. In this life it leads only to the lessening of suffering, because we train ourselves through meditation not to respond to painful feelings with aversion. Though I have bodily infirmities, just as you do, through mindfulness I am just aware of them as bodily infirmities. I feel their pain but I do not hate them or wish them to go away."

Kisa thought for a few moments. "I am not content with this answer, Master," she said, "For it seems to me that your account of the path is false. Certainly it leads to the lessening of suffering, but not to the end of all suffering."

"In future it will lead to the end of all suffering: perhaps after this life, perhaps after many. Human birth is suffering, but this Path leads to the end of rebirth."

"But how do you know this, Master, when you have not yet yourself experienced a state beyond suffering?"

The Buddha was silent.

"How do you know this, reverend sir, when you have not yet yourself experienced a state beyond suffering?"

The Buddha remained silent.

"I insist on an answer, sir. Have you yourself experienced a state beyond suffering? Do you know for sure that such a state exists?"

The Buddha replied at last. “No, I have not experienced such a state. No, I am not sure of the existence of such a state. Human birth is a state of suffering, and we cannot understand or be sure of a state beyond suffering whilst still in a human birth.”

“Then your doctrine is false, Master. Not false all through, I grant you. It is true at the beginning, and true in the middle, but false at the end. I have reached the end: I shall die soon, and it is only truth that concerns me now. Neither the instruction and care of my sisters, nor my own progress in the threefold way, concern me any more. So I must die a householder. I wish to disrobe, Master.”

“So be it. Disrobe if you wish, though your sisters will be dismayed. I fear that a lonely death awaits you, without either your sisters, or any children or lay relatives to attend to you. Such is the death of the proud.”

“Such a death I accept, proud or not, reverend sir.” At that Kisa turned from the gathering and left.

www.ingramcontent.com/pod-product-compliance
Ingram Content Group UK Ltd.
Pitfield, Milton Keynes, MK11 3LW, UK
UKHW020127250726
13967UKWH00002B/515

9 781447 680741